For Now, It Is Night

stories by
HARI KRISHNA KAUL

Translated from the Kashmiri by Kalpana Raina,
Tanveer Ajsi, Gowhar Fazili, and Gowhar Yaqoob

archipelago books

First Archipelago Books Edition, 2024

Library of Congress Cataloging-in-Publication Data available upon request.
ISBN: 9781953861788

Archipelago Books
232 3rd Street #A111
Brooklyn, NY 11215
www.archipelagobooks.org

Distributed by Penguin Random House
www.penguinrandomhouse.com

Cover art by Nilima Sheikh

This work is made possible by the New York State Council on the Arts with the support of
the Office of the Governor and the New York State Legislature. Funding for the publication
of this book was provided by a grant from the Carl Lesnor Family Foundation.

This publication was made possible with support from the National
Endowment for the Arts, the Nimick Forbesway Foundation,
and the Yali Project of Sangham House.

PRINTED IN CANADA

Who knows who will still be here tomorrow
For now, it is night; for now, we wait

—Dina Nath Nadim

Contents

Introduction

G ROWING UP I WAS AWARE THAT MY UNCLE, HARI KRISHNA KAUL, was a short story writer, a playwright, and somewhat of a celebrity in his hometown of Srinagar. That was enough for me and I never attempted to actually read anything he had written. I lived abroad and could not read Kashmiri, the language in which he wrote, although I spoke it quite fluently. It was only in 2009, after Kaul's passing and after I had spent more time in India, that I started to get a sense of his literary achievements. I heard him described, more than once, as one of the best modern short story writers in Kashmiri. I finally persuaded my father to read some of the stories out aloud to me. I knew Kashmiri well enough to immediately understand that Kaul had an impressive eye for detail, a superb command and ease with the language, and a biting wit that both mocked and conveyed empathy for his characters and their situations. Through his work, he examined the minutest details of a very circumscribed Kashmiri Hindu way of life in the last few decades of the twentieth century in old-town Srinagar. This was the world he had grown up in and his ambivalent relationship with it is quite clear in the forewords to his four collections of short stories. There are no grand themes in Kaul's work, but an exploration and ultimately an acceptance of human limitations. He used his personal experiences to explore universal themes of isolation, individual and collective alienation, and the shifting circumstances of a community that went on to experience a significant loss of homeland, culture, and ultimately language.

Hari Krishna Kaul was born in 1934 in Srinagar. He spent his youth and most of his adulthood there, teaching at various academic institutions and leaving only in 1990 in the now well-documented exodus of Hindus from the city. Srinagar and the lives of its citizens are both the focus and the backdrop of Kaul's works, particularly the short stories that span over forty years. The first two collections, *Pata Laraan Parbat* (1972) and *Haalas Chhu Rotul* (1985) include some of his best known and popular works. The last two collections, *Yeth Raazdanay* (1996) and *Zool Apaerim* (2001) were published after Kaul left the Kashmir Valley. The selection of stories in the present Archipelago compilation represents a broad range of both popular and critically acclaimed works from these volumes. The minute observations of a beloved city, the detailed unfolding of ordinary lives lived there, uneasy accommodations between neighbors and communities that eventually end in departures and tenuous adjustments to a new life that was in no way desired; all is catalogued and dissected. Never overtly dogmatic or biased, the simmering political and social conflicts that have dogged Kashmir lurk below the surface of these stories. Kaul's characters, Hindu and Muslim, navigate a common landscape and language but warily, always conscious of the divisions that class and religious identity create.

His characters experience a slow dissolution of personhood as their circumstances, personal and professional, are peeled apart and reveal the void in their lives and the world they inhabit. Time and again, the bulwarks provided by family, jobs, social standing and religion crumble and the individual is left on their own. All this against a backdrop of a festering political and social instability in Kashmir which represents the here and now for these characters. Through humor, compromise and conciliation, they negotiate their ordinary lives in a Kashmir rendered extraordinary by political compulsions. The world outside of Kashmir is alien, rarely named and always represented as "out there" in both a physical and an emotional sense. Mirroring Kaul's own life, the numerous journeys back and forth between these two worlds ultimately end in exile.

In the first story of this collection, "Sunshine," we witness this with the feisty Poshkuj, Kaul's only significant female protagonist. Like the unnamed narrators of many of the later stories, Poshkuj's unravelling of identity and the discomposure this leads to happen subtly. Through bursts of self-reflection peppered with comic descriptions and rendered in biting colloquial prose, we see her brash façade crumble as she struggles to find relevance in her new surroundings. Even on the first reading it becomes obvious why this remains one of Kaul's most iconic stories. The loss of community and the search for meaning that is hinted at in the earlier stories becomes a more direct quest later. Each story builds on this to culminate in "To Rage or To Endure," the last story in this collection. This is a work of astonishingly deft and spare language relying strongly on myth and metaphorical allusions. Here the narrator, unnamed again, stops mining his memories of Kashmir to make that final leap to an existence in exile where relationships and the past are extinguished in order to survive.

After leaving Kashmir in 1990, Kaul was acutely conscious that he had lost his Kashmiri-speaking audience for his television serials and plays. He took refuge in his stories, the stories that in the foreword to *Pata Laraan Parbat* he had called "the children that brought meaning to my meaningless life." He produced two more volumes of stories in Kashmiri but also wrote extensively in Hindi in this period as he tried to carve out a new identity for himself and his writing. His only novel, *Vyath Vyatha,* was published in Hindi in 2005.

It was not initially my intent to translate any of the stories myself. My hope was to bring renewed attention to Kaul's work through fresh contemporary translations and have a new and younger audience engage with them. To that end I enlisted the help of three young scholars and writers who collaborated extensively with me. We encountered significant roadblocks that I had not contemplated. Kaul's own manuscripts and papers were not with his family. Having left Kashmir practically overnight in difficult circumstances these "offspring" were abandoned in the old family home. The magazines in which Kaul published and his books were mostly out of print and any digital archives were inaccessible. The radio and television plays are still unavailable but one of my collaborators was able to locate all four collections of the short stories in the library of Kashmir University. The physical state of these texts was less than ideal. They were in need of preservation. The ink of some pages had faded and entire sentences were sometimes erased, an undesired result of lithographic printing of the earlier volumes. But we managed to have them photocopied. These photocopies were circulated to a small group of Kaul's contemporaries who, along with a handful of younger students and writers, helped us select stories from all four collections.

The three other translators on this project who could read Kashmiri in the Nastaliq script worked from these manuscripts. I had all the selected stories recorded in an attempt to engage members of my family and the extended diaspora who, like me, could not read the script Kaul wrote in. As we were going through our selections, I listened to these stories incessantly. They had a strong dramatic quality, and Kaul's fluid use of the language made them perfect for the audio medium. This was not surprising given the author's copious output of radio and television plays. The stories drew me in and, inspired by the voice recordings, I succumbed to the temptation to translate.

The journey toward an English-language translation was accomplished with multiple translators, all native Kashmiri speakers, but representing a diversity of gender, age, experiences, and religious identity. My knowledge of Kaul, his particular milieu, and the various backstories was enhanced by my collaborators' familiarity with Kashmir, its literary history and landscape, and Kaul's place in it. For all four of us, this was our first experience reading and hearing Kaul and we collectively marveled at his command of the language, his wit and pungent humor, and the complexity of the characters he created. Though fully capable of reading the Nastaliq script, the other translators immersed themselves in the recorded stories as well. Like me, they used the recordings to help capture the orality of Kaul's voice in their translations.

Despite our initial obstacles, the significant disruptions from recent political events in Kashmir and the global pandemic, this project found its way to completion. All these translations are ultimately the result of a collaborative and detailed engagement on the part of the four translators. We allowed each other to work on our separate drafts, but then, over two years of in-person and virtual meetings, interrogated initial assumptions and suggested alternatives that were sometimes accepted and sometimes discarded. This was truly a collective undertaking. We listened, debated, and challenged each other's understanding of the works. We took the process of translation a few levels deeper to bridge and create meaning for ourselves and for a culture and a language that still struggle to find their place in the world.

Kalpana Raina
2022

For Now, It Is Night

Sunshine

NOW THAT SHE HAD ARRIVED IN DELHI, POSHKUJ FELT LIKE she was in a completely different world. She heaved a sigh of relief. Everything else be damned, at least there are no Muslims here. All around me are my own Hindu people. The vegetable man, the baker, the milkman are all Hindus. And what a huge relief it was to be away from that fishwife, her older daughter-in-law. Just the thought of her sent a shiver down Poshkuj's spine. She recalled how often her daughter-in-law would torment her. There was a time when people did not even know Poshkuj's name, and now this shrew had dragged it through the mud. But God has not spared that woman entirely, Poshkuj thought to herself. Gasha and Saiba are born from the same womb. Look how well Saiba is doing here in Delhi, but Gasha can barely feed his family there in Srinagar. And it is all because of the bad luck that shrew brought with her. Poshkuj had already decided that she would not go back to Kashmir, not even in the summer.

It was around ten o'clock in the morning, and Poshkuj went out to the backyard to soak in the sun. Half the yard was paved with bricks, and the other half was a lawn ringed with flowerbeds. The paved area had plants arranged in pots, and creepers and other flowering plants hung like clusters of grapes from the façade of the house.

Saiba or Surendarnath, Poshkuj's younger son, had been allocated a good D-type house in Delhi's Sarojini Nagar. There was a drawing room, a kitchen, and a storeroom on the ground floor. The space in front of the kitchen, furnished with a table and a few chairs, was used as a dining room. Upstairs, there was a bathroom, a toilet and two bedrooms. Saiba and his wife occupied one bedroom; the second room, newly fitted with a bed, was now Poshkuj's. On the top floor was a terrace, with a small room adjoining it.

Surendarnath was back in Delhi after three years. He had gone to England on a scholarship to study, and had then found a job there with the Indian High Commission. Recently transferred to Delhi, he had a good position in the Ministry of External Affairs with a salary of approximately one thousand rupees. He had been married off before leaving for England. Truth be told, Poshkuj regretted that decision. If Saiba were single now, some well-to-do man would have been begging her for an alliance for his daughter. Anyway, what's done is done, she mused. She never spoke of that disappointment to anyone.

Poshkuj lay back in the lawn chair and exposed her arms and legs to the sunshine. She felt the muscles in her back and shoulders relax, and all the accumulated stiffness of Kashmir's winter melted away. She looked up at the sky and admired its deep blue color. Chhoti, her younger daughter-in-law, had hung the washing from the balcony on the second floor, and the clothes were sparkling in the sunlight. Really, these foreign washing machines are amazing. It took Chhoti a mere five minutes to wash all these clothes and look how clean they are. Suddenly, she noticed Chhoti's bra amongst the drying clothes and blushed, wondering what the neighbors who saw this would say. Poshkuj rose from the chair and started to stroll around the yard. A thought suddenly occurred to her, and she started to pick flowers from the garden. She placed the flowers in the folds of her sari and decided that she would ask Chhoti to accompany her to a neighbor-hood temple. They say Birla Mandir is worth seeing, she thought. It wouldn't take more than half an hour, and they could have lunch after they came back. She went inside, put the flowers on the dining table, and sat herself down in a chair. Who knows how long Chhoti will be? She must have been in that bathroom for over an hour. God knows what she is applying to her body. Now that she's in Delhi, she seems to have shed her inhibitions and acquired a brazen new self. Anyway, she's still a thousand times better than that fishwife.

A few minutes later, the door to the bathroom opened and Chhoti came down the stairs briskly. She was wearing a sari and a blouse. Her hair was not combed yet, but she looked so much better than when she had been prancing around in that dressing gown earlier.

"Oh dear! What have you done Mataji?" Chhoti exclaimed when she saw the plucked flowers on the dining table.

Poshkuj was petrified and realized instantly that she had done something terribly wrong.

"Why did you pick the flowers from the garden, particularly the hollyhocks?" Chhoti asked, half plaintive, half angry.

Poshkuj was stung by her daughter-in-law's tone. After all, it was just a matter of a few flowers, she thought. And why was Chhoti being so pretentious? In Kashmir I was "Kakin", and now in Delhi I am "Mataji"? What nonsense! But she swallowed her anger and replied softly.

"I thought we could go to the temple."

"Well, you should have asked me first. There are no temples in this neighborhood, or even nearby. Ashoka Hotel and Chanakyapuri are close by, but no temples," said Chhoti.

"What are those places?" Poshkuj asked.

"You wouldn't understand," said Chhoti. "Let's go outside and sit in the sun."

Poshkuj felt a wave of anger sweep over her body. This idiot's daughter understands, and I don't? I have to stand up for myself and talk back to her now, otherwise I won't have the right to speak in the future.

"You think I'm stupid," said Poshkuj. "I know that Birla Mandir, that one which people visit from all over the country, it's in this city."

"Birla Mandir? Why that's very far, even further than Connaught Place and Gole Market," said Chhoti.

This, too, sounded false to Poshkuj. From the terrace yesterday, in the direction of the setting sun, she had seen a temple-like building with blue domes in the distance, and had convinced herself that it was Birla Mandir. She stood her ground and confronted her daughter-in-law. "Then what is that temple with the blue domes? You know, the one that is visible from the terrace? Even the maid said it was Birla Mandir."

"Mataji, what does the maid know?" countered Chhoti. "That building is neither a temple nor a mosque. It is the Pakistani Embassy. The office of Pakistan."

Poshkuj could not stomach the condescension in Chhoti's voice. What kind of a fool does this woman take me for? How brazenly she lies! In Kashmir, despite all the Muslims around, no one speaks of Pakistan openly. So how can there be an office of Pakistan here, in Delhi, where only Hindus live? What an outrageous lie! But I don't like confrontations with people who curse or argue for no reason. What if she responds like that shrew, my other daughter-in-law? I won't be able to defend myself. I should just stay quiet.

It was around noon, and Chhoti turned on the stove in the kitchen and made the rotis. She reheated the vegetables she had cooked earlier and put them on the dining table. She took out a few glasses for water, put some sliced onions in a small plate and squeezed lemon juice over them. Poshkuj understood that a meal was being prepared.

"I am not going to eat lunch," she said dismissively.

"But why not? Are you fasting today?" asked Chhoti.

"Why would I fast? Just put the plates away and give me my food in that small basin. I'll sit on the floor and eat." Poshkuj went upstairs to her room, brought out the torn rug that had protected her bedroll on the journey from Kashmir, and spread it on the floor in front of the dining table. Chhoti took all of this in quietly and gave Poshkuj her food in the small basin. The old woman took a towel from her petticoat pocket, spread it on the floor, placed her glass on it, and holding the bowl in her lap, started to eat cheerfully.

Chhoti took her own lunch up to her bedroom. After an hour or so, she came down again. She had changed her clothes, and this time, she had combed and braided her hair as well.

"Mataji, I am going out to meet Miss Kapoor. I'll be back by about three o'clock."

Poshkuj remained quiet, but her silence did not discourage Chhoti who, with a quick glance at her watch, stepped out. Poshkuj was slightly dejected, but felt that she had no right to stop her daughter-in-law who could do as she pleased. She went out into the backyard again, where the warmth of the sun cheered her up.

One could die for this sunshine. This is truly the only worthwhile thing in Delhi. She raised her sari slightly and scratched her right leg. She looked at her chapped skin and cursed the cold of Kashmir that was so hard on one's hands and feet. Reflecting on the weather, she remembered her grandson, Bittě. Poor boy! How miserable he is, with his chilblains. How many times I told that monster mother of his that her son's feet needed attention. Make sure he wears socks and fur-lined shoes, I said. But would that woman listen to me? Of course, fur-lined shoes are expensive and Gasha barely manages to get by. He doesn't even have an overcoat for himself and shivers in the cold. She sighed. It's all a matter of one's fate.

Poshkuj surveyed the neighboring houses. It was quiet everywhere. It's as if no one is around, or they're all dead. Everyone feels like a stranger here. I miss the friendly chatter amongst neighbors. But even if I were to talk to these people, would I understand the language they speak? Look at the strange names these women have. Mrs. Jain, Mrs. Sundaram, Mrs. Prakash and Mrs. Whatever. That Sikh lady in the house next door – she probably has daughters and daughters-in-law my age, but she calls herself Mrs. Khem Singh. What kind of names are these? Delhi is all right, but really, I don't see what's so great about it.

She heard the sound of a scooter engine being turned off and realized that Saiba, her son, was home. Yes, it was Saiba, wheeling his scooter in.

He asked, "How have you been today?"

"I've been well. God bless you," said Poshkuj.

Saiba ran upstairs to his room but came down immediately.

"Where is she?" he asked.

"Oh, she's gone to meet Mrs. Kapoor," was her response.

"Which Mrs. Kapoor?"

"You know, the one with the wild hair, who is fair and slim? That one."

"I'm sorry, I don't know who you're talking about."

"You know the one I mean," said Poshkuj.

Saiba burst out laughing. "That's not what you said. This one is Miss Kapoor, Mr. Kapoor's daughter. You said Mrs. Kapoor. That means Mr. Kapoor's wife."

"As if I care. How am I supposed to understand these differences?" said Poshkuj.

"Well, if you live here, you will have to understand these subtleties," replied Saiba, going up the stairs again as he tried to end the conversation.

"Why is Chhoti so friendly with this Kapoor person?" Poshkuj asked. "I don't like her, and I don't care for her ways."

"You're wrong, she is a good person. Besides, we have to look after our own interests, no?"

"What do you mean?"

"What I mean is that her father is a senior officer in All India Radio, and Chhoti is looking for a job there."

Poshkuj was surprised. "You mean you're going to make your wife work? Isn't your salary enough?"

"It's not a question of money," said Saiba. "Chhoti is lonely here, and a job will keep her busy. Anyway, what's wrong with saving a little more money? We also have a lot of expenses. We have a radio, but no TV. We have a scooter but not a car."

"You are too greedy," Poshkuj shot back.

Saiba laughed and turned away. He saw the old torn rug that was still spread out on the floor.

"Who put this old rug here?" he asked.

Poshkuj sensed Saiba's anger and quietly said, "I did. I can't eat sitting at the dining table."

Saiba said nothing. After a while, when Chhoti returned, the two of them had a brief conversation. They had their tea, called for a taxi, and along with Poshkuj, went to Chandni Chowk. There, they bought a steel plate, a low wooden seat, a few pairs of slippers, an embroidered sari, and a small statue of Lord Shiva.

That night, Poshkuj was served dinner in the new steel plate.

Poshkuj could not sleep a wink. So many different thoughts raced through her mind. I suppose they intend to buy a car. What good fortune this younger daughter-in-law of mine has! Well, at least her good luck has rubbed off on her husband as well. Otherwise, she could have been like that wretch in Kashmir who has brought her poor husband nothing but misfortune. I wonder if Gasha has bought a bicycle . . . He said he would, if he could get one on instalments. He must get tired, walking from Rainawari to his office.

Oh, this quilt feels too heavy for these warm Delhi nights. I wonder how cold Srinagar is. I should tell Saiba to write to his brother and caution him not to stay out late at night. Tutoring that girl in Jawahar Nagar is not worth it. God forbid, if something were to happen to him . . . What would happen to all of us?

What a lot of things were being sold in Chandni Chowk! So many clothes that would have been good for Bittĕ. I would have bought something for him if I had money of my own. But I am sure I will go back to Chandni Chowk soon – then, I'll buy a shirt and shorts and a hockey stick for Bittĕ. I'll probably have to buy bangles for the neighbor's daughter too, and of course, some ordinary sari for that wretch of a daughter-in-law. Well, Saiba will take good care of me if I'm lucky enough to stay alive. He promised to take me to Haridwar next month. His poor father had always wanted to see Haridwar, but even in death he only managed to make it to Shadipur. Gasha never could have managed the five or six hundred rupees it would have cost. If Saiba had been here at the time, it would have been a different story.

And what do you know – there are Muslims in this city after all. Those burqa-clad women were strolling about so casually in Chandni Chowk. I wonder if they fear living in Delhi just as we fear living in Kashmir. But we haven't been killed there, so why would they be attacked here? Still, how do you smother the fear in your heart?

Just then, Poshkuj heard the door to Saiba's room open and someone walked quickly across the cement floor. She recognized the footsteps. After a while, she heard the toilet being flushed. Of course, Chhoti has an upset stomach. What did she expect after eating that bowl full of lentils with her rice? The sound of the flush probably woke up the whole neighborhood. She might as well have broadcast her condition from the radio. After all, isn't that where she is going to work now?

As dawn approached, Poshkuj got out of bed. She went to the toilet and then took a quick bath. Back in her room, she wrapped a blanket closely around herself. She placed the statue of Lord Shiva in front of herself and started to sing hymns, even ones that she only half remembered, like the Shiva Mahimna Stotra. After her prayers, she went up to the terrace to sit in the morning sun. The Delhi sky felt wide open, unlike the sky in Kashmir that was hemmed in by the surrounding mountains. Maybe it's because of these open skies that the people here seem broad-minded. It feels good to bathe every day. Just at that moment, Saiba called to her and she went downstairs.

All the paraphernalia of breakfast – teacups, saucers, bread and eggs – had been laid out on the table. Saiba, in a dressing gown, was sitting in one of the chairs, reading a newspaper. Chhoti emerged from the kitchen with a teapot in her hand. She, too, was wearing a dressing gown and had a red handkerchief tied around her hair. She put the teapot down on the table, and took the butter and strawberry jam out of the fridge and spread them on slices of bread. Poshkuj drank her tea along with a few slices of bread. The young couple ate eggs. Poshkuj watched Chhoti eat her egg, and again she was reminded of her grandson. How skinny he is. He doesn't even get a cup of milk there. If his mother had sent him here with me, he would have put on some weight.

Saiba went up to his room after breakfast. Chhoti cleared the table, put the dirty dishes in the kitchen sink for the maid, and followed her husband up the stairs. After a short while, both of them came down, dressed and ready to go out. Poshkuj looked them over.

"I am going to work and will drop Chhoti off at the market," said Saiba, as he wheeled his scooter out. Chhoti sat behind him, with her right hand on his shoulder. As she watched them drive away, Poshkuj thought again about Gasha. I wonder if he has bought the bicycle.

If only I could send him the little money I have, it might help. She was thinking about this when Miss Kapoor suddenly appeared in the doorway.

"Namaskar, is Mrs. Bhan at home?" Miss Kapoor asked in Hindi.

In her broken Hindi, Poshkuj said that her daughter-in-law had gone to the market to buy meat and told Miss Kapoor to sit and wait. Miss Kapoor smiled in a way that Poshkuj did not like and brushed past the old lady, going straight into the drawing room as if this were her own home. "The cheek!" Poshkuj shrugged dramatically and went out to the yard to sit in the sun.

When Chhoti came back, Poshkuj informed her that Mrs. Kapoor was waiting inside.

"Mataji," Chhoti admonished her, "not Mrs. Kapoor, please call her Miss Kapoor."

"Whatever," said Poshkuj. "I was trying to be polite and she made fun of me."

"I'm sure you're mistaken. She would not behave like that," said Chhoti as she went into the drawing room.

Poshkuj was hurt by her daughter-in-law's refusal to take her seriously. Why did I even start this? God knows what my son and his wife see in this woman. But of course, they are trying to get her father to help them. Miss Kapoor, indeed! I'm sure she's slept around quite a bit in her time, and she still calls herself *Miss*. Poshkuj shrugged to show her contempt.

The warmth of the sun made Poshkuj sleepy. She heard peals of laughter from the drawing room and suspected that Chhoti and

Miss Kapoor were making fun of her. She cringed. Perhaps it wasn't going to be possible to stay in Delhi much longer, she thought. She would leave for Kashmir soon if she could find someone to travel with. And if she could, she would take baskets full of this sunshine back with her.

The Saint and the Witch

Tara Chand died at five-thirty in the morning. The news reached Ram Joo's house at seven, and he left Jawahar Nagar immediately for Bane Mohalla with his wife, Sonmaal and sister, Hei Batein.

"How lucky he is to die like this," Ram Joo said as he walked along. "No pain, no sickness. I'd met him only two days ago at Habba Kadal and we'd had a long chat. He'd said, 'Once the weather improves, I'll come to Jawahar Nagar to spend a day with you.' Truly, people do not realize that death is always with them." He sighed.

"His life ended, but he left that poor woman behind to be pushed around," Sonmaal said.

"In these times, even your own children don't care for you. How can an adopted child be expected to? Lord, keep me well while I'm alive and take me to your home in good health." She wiped her tears with the edge of her headscarf.

'That poor man was so virtuous. He helped relatives and strangers alike. He moved in important circles and was well respected," Ram Joo said.

"He was very handsome," said Sonmaal. "He looked wonderful in that parrot-green turban, beige achkan, white-pleated pajamas, and slip-on shoes. His shoes were always polished."

"You could call him a dandy," said Ram Joo light-heartedly. "We all know how elegantly he tied his turban. When I tied my nephew Gasha's turban on his wedding day, that wretch unwound it saying that he wouldn't go to his bride's home unless Tara Chand retied it."

"He was so pious. Word has it that he would go to Hari Parbat even in this condition." Sonmaal changed the subject.

"Not only that, he would spend every Saturday night at Chakreshwari. He would visit Kheer Bhawani every month on the eighth night of the moon," Ram Joo added.

"One day, I heard him singing hymns at Tul Mul. His voice was so sweet, it sounded like bells tinkling," Sonmaal said.

"He truly was a most pious man, quite exemplary. He took pleasure in worldly things, but rose to mystical heights as well. He would often mutter esoteric prayers under his breath," Ram Joo continued.

"And all of that served him well at the time of his death. As they say, great souls depart this world without suffering," Sonmaal said.

"Such a death deserves to be celebrated," Ram Joo said.

Hei Batein listened quietly to the conversation between her brother and her sister-in-law, but she was becoming more and more agitated. It surprised her that they hadn't stopped talking for even a moment. Why were they going to Bane Mohalla so eagerly as if to a feast? Tara Chand had died suddenly, and they didn't seem to care. She had been struck speechless. If she had known that Tara Chand would die so soon, she would have gone to him, fallen at his feet and begged for forgiveness. She would have confessed her heart had been so full of sin at that time, that she had almost destroyed the forbearance of even a great sage like Tara Chand. But sadly, he had not given Hei Batein a chance to repent. His death pierced her heart like an arrow, leaving a wound that would not heal in this lifetime.

"Tara Chand was truly a saint," Ram Joo praised the dead man again.

"He certainly was," Sonmaal said. "Pure of heart, untouched by evil, like the king of gods. His wife was ugly and unworthy, and yet he put up with her without complaint."

"Tarawati was certainly not the wife he deserved," Ram Joo said.

"What a wife! Stupid and just plain awkward," Sonmaal said.

"Well, she's the one who will suffer the most now. Who knows if Nath will let her stay with them and take care of her?"

"She gave him no comfort. Now she'll reap as she has sown."

"There is not much affection between parents and adopted children."

"Don't say that," Sonmaal reprimanded her husband. "Nath Ji is a real gem. His wife Shanti is also very loving. Neither husband nor wife will allow Tarawati to lift a finger. One's own children can suck the life out of you." She tightened the sash around her tunic.

"Tarawati raised him like her own, didn't she?"

"I know that!" Sonmaal snapped at her husband. "I haven't lived my whole life in a Jawahar Nagar bungalow. We lived in Tara Chand's house as tenants for eleven years. I know every bit of it. I have never seen Tarawati smile. God gave her what she deserved. Even a bitch is preferable to a barren woman."

"Come, now. That's none of our concern. It was Tara Chand who stayed in touch with us. Now that he's gone, that chapter is over."

"He was someone who kept up relations. He was courteous and hospitable." Sonmaal wasn't done speaking. "But that wretched woman, whenever she saw a guest approaching, her face would crumple as if she were mourning the death of her father."

"Tara Chand lived a good life full of pleasure. He prospered and let others benefit as well. He was a revenue officer at a time when that was a coveted job. He thrived in every position he took on, and retired before democracy ushered in a new order."

"This man who so loved pleasure had but one sorrow."

"Actually, Tarawati is not so bad . . . apart from being a bit short."

"It is not just about her looks. She's a monster," Sonmaal said. "Not everyone can be beautiful like a princess. She knew very well that her husband was particular about cleanliness, but she never paid any attention to her appearance. She wouldn't even bother to wash her face. She'd sit at the window all day long in a dirty patched tunic. Her hair was always a tangled mess. She looked like a witch."

"But Tara Chand never complained to anyone," said Ram Joo.

"Never," agreed Sonmaal.

"He cared for her, unlike most husbands these days."

"He was a saint."

"That witch destroyed him and ruined his life!"

Tara Chand's life had indeed been wasted. Hei Batein had realized this before anyone else, perhaps because her own youthful desires had remained unfulfilled. She had been sixteen when she married. Her husband had died a mere five years later. In the five years of her married life, she had spent three and a half years at her mother's house. That was almost thirty-two years ago, and today she couldn't even remember the face of her short-lived husband. If she tried hard to recall him, the faint image of an eighteen- or nineteen-year-old Brahmin boy, thin and shy, appeared before her eyes. He would follow her when she climbed upstairs to fetch rice and spices from the storeroom, but run away with his tail between his legs when he heard his mother call out to him, "Damodaro!" His mother was cruel. Forget letting husband and wife sleep in their own bedroom, she wouldn't even let them speak to one another. When Hei Batein would come back from her mother's to her husband's house, his mother would send him to his grandparents' house the very same day. She worried that she would lose her grip over her son. But in spite of all her efforts, she had lost him forever after five years.

She outlived him by barely a year. Hei Batein had been distraught for a long time.

After her mother-in-law died, her brother brought her to his home. For about a year, she was treated well, but soon her sister-in-law made her do all the household chores. Perhaps God had brought her into the world for this purpose alone, she thought. Heartbroken, she began to work tirelessly in her brother's house. Shortly after this, Ram Joo got into a feud with his uncles and moved with his family into Tara Chand's house. Tara Chand gave Hei Batein a new lease on life. He stopped going out to meet people after work. Instead, he would read the Ramayana, the Mahabharata, the Bhagavata and the Shiva Purana to her. He also bought her the Gita and the Hanuman Chalisa. Instead of sweeping the stairs, she would go to the Shiva temple with her offerings. Like Tara Chand, she too began to fast on the eighth, eleventh and fifteenth days of the moon. During these days of fasting, she would cook the ritual foods for Tara Chand. She prepared puffed rice, fried potatoes, pakoras, halwa, tapioca pudding and brought him boiled milk to drink. She ate only after serving him. Tarawati probably did not like Hei Batein's intrusion, but she never complained.

Hei Batein accompanied Tara Chand on many of his pilgrimages. She travelled with him to Tul Mul every month on the eighth day of the moon. Once, Tara Chand even took her to Bhawan to perform the memorial rites for her husband Damodar who had died so young. When they heard that a sadhu of great spiritual power had come to Chandigam, Tara Chand took Hei Batein along with him to visit the holy man. They spent a night at the sadhu's ashram, then set out on foot for Sogam the next day at two in the afternoon. A cold shiver ran down Hei Batein's spine as she remembered that day. Without warning, it had started to rain heavily on their way home. They got drenched and couldn't get a bus from Sogam to Srinagar. It turned out that Tara Chand knew a government official in the area who was away in Srinagar. He asked the caretaker of the official's house to let them stay there. The caretaker started a fire so that both Tara Chand and Hei Batein could warm themselves and dry their clothes. At around five in the afternoon, Tara Chand went out to buy mutton. He asked the caretaker for some rice, spices and oil. Hei Batein cooked the food in the kitchen, and after eating at nine or ten at night, she prepared the official's bed for Tara Chand. She pulled out a couple of blankets for herself but couldn't get to sleep until late. It rained incessantly, and that July night felt as cold as December. After tossing and turning for a long time, when Hei Batein could bear it no longer, she got up and slowly slipped under Tara Chand's quilt. As she was about to put her left arm around his shoulder, he awoke. When he realized that Hei Batein was in his bed, he stood up. He washed his hands and face and sat down to meditate. Hei Batein's whole being was flooded with shame and she rushed into the kitchen. She wanted the earth to open up and swallow her. Her eyes were swollen with tears. For a long time, she could not face Tara Chand. Thankfully, they left Tara Chand's house for Jawahar Nagar soon after. Before moving out, Ram Joo and his family had a bitter fight with Tarawati, and they didn't speak to each other for three years.

A long time had passed since then. Hei Batein was nearing fifty now. She had prepared herself several times to visit Tara Chand to ask him for forgiveness. But she hadn't had the strength to face him and an opportunity had not presented itself. Now, as they made their way to the dead man's house, she felt that the distance from Jawahar Nagar to Bane Mohalla was growing and feared that Tara Chand's body might be gone by the time they got there.

Ram Joo, Sonmaal and Hei Batein reached Bane Mohalla at eight. Tara Chand's body had not yet been taken away. In the courtyard, a bier had been prepared for the corpse. The many people gathered there were sitting on reed mats and praising the departed soul. Ram Joo joined the men while Sonmaal and Hei Batein entered the house. When Tarawati saw them enter, she and a few other women began to lament and wail loudly. Sonmaal covered Tarawati's mouth with her hand to calm her down. Hei Batein didn't sit next to Tarawati. Instead, she went out to where Tara Chand's body lay on a pile of hay. She touched his feet and cried aloud: "O father, O brother, O guru!" Then, she prostrated herself and said quietly, "I was blinded by darkness, forgive me my sins. This life has been wasted. I hope that my next life won't be like this one. Forgive me."

Tara Chand's body was lifted on to the lavishly decorated bier at around eleven. Before it was carried out from the courtyard, the corpse was covered with an exquisite shawl. Wailing, Tarawati followed the funeral procession to the end of the lane from where some women walked her back to the house. She entered and sat in grief-stricken silence. Then she turned to the women around her. "Please don't kill me. For fifty years I kept this secret. Now that he is not here, I am telling you . . . I am like a seven-year-old girl, I am pure."

Hei Batein was shaken to her core when she heard this. The events of the past made more sense now and what had been said before took on a new meaning. She got up and embraced Tarawati and both of them began to wail.

Complicit

Hazrat, it was probably one o'clock in the morning, and I was dead tired, out cold, when my wife suddenly woke me up. I was outraged. *Why wouldn't I be?*

I cursed her and wanted to know why she had disturbed me.

"There is a lot of noise outside; perhaps there's a fire somewhere," she replied.

Hearing this, my anger dissipated. I got out of bed, put on my pajamas, slid my feet into a pair of worn-out slippers and promptly made my way towards the market. Outside, I saw a large crowd of people raising a ruckus. However, it didn't seem that a fire had broken out; I was relieved. *Why wouldn't I be?*

Rubbing my eyes, I moved closer to the crowd and realized that they had caught a thief and were beating him mercilessly. Some were hitting him, others kicking him, and a few more were punching him. In the midst of all of this, some bastard headbutted the thief so hard that he fell to the ground like a cucumber from its vine. I thought he was done for. I confronted the crowd. *I had to.*

"Hey, you scoundrels," I said, "do you want to kill this man? If you caught him stealing, hand him over to the police. Who gave you the right to lynch him?"

Hearing me, the thief suddenly sprang back to life. It turned out he was faking it all along. He showered blessings on me: "May God bless you, grant you good health, and…"

Hey you, why are you sitting down with a book now? Am I talking nonsense? Am I ranting here? So what if you have a class to teach, do you really need to look over your lessons right now? I have been teaching for fifteen years, and I swear not once have I crammed with a book before a class. Never felt the need to! Come on, close that book. Yes, just like that.

What was I saying? Right, I told the crowd to hand the thief over to the police. Some agreed with my suggestion, and some did not. But eventually, everyone figured it was a good idea to let them handle the matter. A few people went to the police station and came back with a couple of policemen, who took the thief away. The crowd dispersed, and everybody went home.

About a week later, while I was getting ready for college, a few people from the neighborhood showed up at my house. I asked why they had come, and one of them spoke up, "Nabbe Sahib, you had asked us to turn the thief over to the police, but a week has passed, and no action has been taken yet. You have no idea, these thieves are often in cahoots with the police.

I paused for a moment and then asked who the officer in charge of the police station was.

They told me it was a certain Bashir Ahmed of Kawdore. I suspected this was probably the same Bashe Lal who had been my classmate until the second year of middle school at Dilawar Bagh. It is extremely embarrassing to talk about this with Raina Sahib here, but Rahim Gore, a few other boys, and I used to take Bashe Lal behind the bushes at Monglun every Friday.

Anyway, that very evening, I went to the police station. To be honest, Bashe Lal was extremely hospitable. He served me tea and treated me to Bakir Khani and some eggs. Obviously, he had not forgotten our childhood friendship. After finishing our tea, I got to the heart of the matter straightaway.

"This is all well and good; you caught the thief, but what proof do you have?" Bashe Lal asked. "We cannot start any proceedings unless we have some concrete proof."

I reminded him that there were plenty of witnesses to this incident.

"Having witnesses alone is not enough; we also require solid proof," he retorted. "Here is a suggestion," he continued, "ask your neighbors to bring some valuables to the station, a shawl perhaps, a suit, some jewelry, a transistor, a watch, ten or twenty kilos of copperware. Then, we can claim that the thief was caught with these objects in his possession. Our case will be stronger, and the thief will be punished. After that, people can take their things back."

Bashe Lal's plan made sense to me, and I relayed it to the neighborhood folks. By the way, I forgot to tell you that as I was leaving Bashe Lal's office, I noticed the thief relaxing on a mat on the veranda with two policemen, relishing fries. They were gossiping about a certain Aziz Rather's daughter-in-law. As soon as the thief saw me, he stood up with great deference as if I were his brother-in-law and started offering me blessings again, "May my God bless you with infinite happiness. If it were not for you, those scoundrels would have torn me apart and fed me piece by piece to the dogs."

Assuming a new sense of confidence, I told him it was my civic duty. I must admit here that watching them relish those fries made my mouth water. I briefly contemplated asking for some but realized it would be beneath me. They might think that teachers are no better than beggars. So, I suppressed the urge. *Why wouldn't I?*

When I shared Bashe Lal's plan with the neighbors, they were astounded. One of them said, "Nabbe Sahib, excuse my bluntness, but either you are an idiot, or you think we are gullible. When you were in Islamabad a while ago, we had caught another thief and similarly handed him over to the police. At that time, too, Bashir Ahmed had asked us to bring a similar set of objects. But the thief was not punished, nor did we get our things back. Bashir Ahmed kept everything for himself. These police officers have a habit of usurping what is not theirs. What these scoundrels were saying rang true. *How could it not?*

I immediately went back to the police station and confronted Bashe Lal. Cursing him, I asked how could he have fallen so low. "You'd be better off begging." In my heart though, I thought, hey, if you want a shawl or a transistor, come with me to Monglun, and I will make it worth your while. But Bashe Lal vehemently rejected this allegation and said that it was the thief who took those objects.

"What nonsense. How is that even possible?" I asked.

"It is not nonsense at all. The case against the thief did not hold up in court. The law has so many nuances," Bashe Lal explained. "The judge agreed with the thief's claim that those were his own belongings. What else could we have done?"

What is it, Nama Singh? What are they saying? Is it time for my class? Did you hear the bell ring? Alright, tell them I am giving them a break today. But they must maintain order and stay out of the principal's sight. What else are they asking now? A list of probable questions for the exam? What will they do with it? Why don't they show us how brilliant they are during the examination itself and not bother me right now?

Hazrat, I had the privilege of witnessing the remarkable efficiency of our examination system when I was recently appointed the Deputy Superintendent for the M.A. exams. I would not have accepted, but the principal insisted. The superintendent was one Mr. Pipli. Why use his real name here? Jawaharlal Ji is smirking. I think he has figured out who I am referring to. Anyway, just ignore that.

Alright, good health to all of you.

This Mr. Pipli I was talking about was being very strict and not allowing any student to even look sideways. Yet, right in front of him, in the first row, a few boys were cheating brazenly from open textbooks. Mr. Pipli was a cowardly Kashmiri Brahmin, after all, who was afraid of those Muslim boys. I found this favoritism highly disagreeable and unjust. So I whispered to the other students, "Why don't you also take advantage of this opportunity? Are those boys his sons-in-law, but not you?"

Emboldened by my support, the students quickly pulled bits of paper and books from their pockets and started cheating with no compunction. They had come fully prepared but lacked courage. Mr. Pipli disapproved and protested, "This is not appropriate!"

"It was inappropriate until now. As teachers, we must treat every student equally, and as for the rules, we shall follow them to the letter," I responded. He did not pursue the matter further.

For the next three hours, I repeated the following warning thirteen times: "Anyone caught cheating or attempting to cheat, or anybody trying to help or seek help from one another, will be disqualified for one to five years." Making this announcement repeatedly was my duty. After every announcement, I would pass one boy's paper to another and help other boys with questions to which I somewhat knew the answers. Well, the examination went splendidly. *Why wouldn't it?*

There was no noise or fuss at our examination center. Our boys continued working quietly. The university officials were also very pleased with us. But this was not the case with other centers.

What do you think, Raina Sahib? You likely find it disgraceful,

don't you? But you didn't think that last year, when your own daughter had to appear for her chemistry practical, and you arrived at the
examination hall at Nawa Kadal College quite early to find out what
compound she had to analyze. Does that ring a bell? I thought so.
One tends to forget such incidents. Anyway, let's move on. At the
end of the day, we all are complicit. When our political leaders get
elected through questionable means, how can we blame those poor
fellows? Oh dear, Raina Sahib appears to be upset. Let's forget all
this. Let's get back to Bashe Lal's story, which I bet you were enjoy-
ing. Where was I? Those rascals distracted me with their demands.

Yes, now I recall. Bashe Lal informed me that the court had
ordered the stolen property to be given to the thief. He also requested
that I relay this information to my neighbors, which I did. They gathered some items and dropped them off at the police station. But what
sort of items, you may ask? Well, they included a broken pick, a torn
phĕrăn, and a cooking pot without a bottom, among other things.

A few days later, Bashe Lal came by to inform me that the thief
would be tried in court the following day and asked if I could find the
time to attend. I told him I would try.

Nama Singh, get me a glass of water.

The next day, the college closed at noon. Siddiq Sahib and Dhar
Sahib had the Muslim boys submit a request to the principal to get
the day off to attend the Urs of Dastgir Sahib, a local Sufi saint. So
the college closed early. The students went to the movies. Siddiq
Sahib visited his private students, tuitions he pocketed on the side,

and Dhar Sahib went home to take a nap – or do whatever else, only God and his wife could tell you. As for the other teachers, they skedaddled. With Bashe Lal's words in my head, I set off for the court.

Raina Sahib, we really need new glasses for the staffroom. It is embarrassing to use the ones we have. Don't we professors deserve better?

When I arrived, the judge was hearing this very case. Bashe Lal was making a statement. The judge was flipping through a book of pictures and shaking his head from time to time, indicating that he was listening attentively. The thief was standing on one side of the courtroom with two policemen. Therefore, I went to the other side, where a clerk was trying to extract a bribe from a litigant. I thought my presence there might disrupt things, so I stepped back. That's when the thief noticed me and greeted me with great respect. You might find it hard to believe, but no one had ever shown me such deference before.

After greeting me, the thief reached into his pocket and offered me a pack of Gold Flake cigarettes. I was embarrassed. *Why wouldn't I be?*

But then I thought, at least I would save some money on cigarettes, and besides, my friends would be jealous when they saw me smoking Gold Flake.

I went outside to smoke. I was blowing out smoke rings from a long drag when I felt someone's hand on my shoulder. It was Bashe Lal. He pulled me aside and said, "I believe you get along well with this thief. Tell him to give me two hundred rupees, and we will settle the case."

I thought it best to resolve the matter in this manner. Bashe Lal, after all, was a dear friend, and the thief, too, was not such a bad guy.

About half an hour later, when the policemen escorted the thief out, I whispered Bashe Lal's proposition to him. That scoundrel deviously replied, "If he gives me three hundred rupees instead, I may let him off. And only because of my great esteem for you." I was stunned. *Why wouldn't I be?*

To this day, I haven't figured out what harm he could have done to Bashe Lal.

And what then? What did you think was going to happen? This isn't an Amin Kamil or Bansi Nirdosh story, with a dramatic twist at the end to astound everyone. As far as I know, Bashe Lal and the thief did not come to any resolution. It would have been good if they had because I might have benefitted too. I don't know if they reached an agreement at all. A few days later, my family and I moved to Jawahar Nagar. That's the whole story. Screw them both. Do you have a cigarette?

Twins

SAHIB SEEMED STARTLED WHEN HE SAW ME. HE DREW BACK A little. My hunch was right. I thought it best not to waste time, so I quickly joined my palms and said respectfully, "Sir, I'm not him. I'm his brother. We were born twins, that's why we look alike." He studied me from head to toe. My attractive appearance, my clothes, my smile, and my humble demeanor convinced him that I was not that wretched fellow. We were both silent for a while, and then he asked, "Where is he now?"

"Sir, he passed away few days ago."

This news seemed to lift his spirits and he burst out laughing. I also smiled a little. Then suddenly, he turned serious. I too put on a serious face.

"He was stubborn, but we must admit that his pen carried weight."

"Sir, you might be right, but what good was that?" I asked. "He made us destitute. Sir, it is generous of you not to criticize him, but I must tell you – he was a vagabond who ruined his life and made his family suffer. You said his pen carried weight, sir. He suffered from the same delusion. If that was true, he would have received awards from government institutions. We live in a democracy now, not under a dictatorship. These days, awards are given after assessing a person's abilities and are based on the merits of their work."

Sahib laughed. I also smiled a little. "Does your family miss him?'" he asked after a short silence.

"No, sir, not at all. Father was already upset with him. But mother was very fond of him. She loved everything about him. When he would finally come home after wandering around all night, he would find her waiting for him with a bowl of food. But eventually, she also gave up."

"Did you ever talk to him?"

"A lot, sir, but it was useless. As Lal Děd said: do not waste words of wisdom on a fool."

Sahib rose quickly. I too got up. He went inside. I sat back on the sofa.

I had counseled my brother on many occasions. I had lectured him at length. I would summon all my knowledge and all my wisdom to persuade him. He would listen to me in silence, only to laugh it all off in the end. It made me feel inferior and made my words sound hollow. Eventually, I decided to get rid of him. I would never flourish otherwise. Several times, I thought of strangling him, but whenever I stood before him, my strength ebbed and I was drenched in sweat.

Something odd happened a few days ago, though. He came home at midnight, tears streaming down his cheeks. He hugged me the moment he saw me and sobbed inconsolably. I wiped his tears and asked him what was wrong. His voice was strained when he replied, "You made fun of my clothes and my vagabond way of life all the time, but I never took it badly. I always stood on my own two feet. I was neither helpless nor dependent. I had entrusted a hundred thousand rupees to someone, but today I found out that he's bankrupt. Totally broke. Maybe he was always penniless, and I mistook him for a millionaire. Basically, I am ruined."

I smelled his breath. Perhaps he'd had an extra drink that day, which is why the wretch was talking of lakhs and crores. Then he became even more incoherent and began to ramble. He talked about communism, then switched to the music halls of Czechoslovakia. He boasted about socialism and then he blathered on about income tax. He delivered a sermon on Gandhi's non-violence and spoke of smoke rising from the cotton mills of Ahmedabad. Finally, he collapsed, exhausted, and fell to the floor with a thud.

This is the moment, I thought. I steeled myself, sought courage from God and strangled him in the dead of night. His eyes popped out and he quickly turned cold. In the morning, everyone saw his corpse lying in the room. His bulging eyes were horrifying. When we closed his eyes before covering his face, two big tears rolled out of them.

Sahib came back into the drawing room. I got up. He sat down. I also sat down.

"What were you thinking about?" he asked.

"Nothing, sir. I was just admiring your taste. The color of these walls, the design of the sofas, the choice of artwork – sir, you yourself are a great artist!"

He laughed. I also smiled a little.

"I am sure you too must have a well-decorated drawing room."

"How I wish, sir. But because of that miserable fellow, we live in a hovel."

"For now, you can submit an application for a plot of land. Leave the rest to God."

Deep inside, I knew that God was with me. Finally, I confessed to Sahib that I was also writing a book and that I would like him to write the foreword.

Sahib laughed. I also smiled a little.

I left there happy. My heart assured me that God would be on my side. But I was worried that the wretch's ghost would not let me live, prosper, or write in peace. They say that if someone is killed like this, their ghost torments even innocent people until the Day of Judgement.

Tomorrow – A Never-Ending Story

A S THE BOYS BEGAN TO ENTER THEIR CLASSROOMS AFTER PRAYER, Sulleh of Class IV said to Makhan, "Learnt the tables for Neelkanth, bugger?"

"No. You?"

"Tried, but couldn't memorize them."

"What do we do now? He is a real pain in the neck." Makhan's face grew pale.

Sulleh laughed it off and quietly slipped something to Makhan. "Here, rub this on your hands, bugger."

"What is it?"

"Sheep tallow. Rub it on your hands and the caning won't hurt."

"Swear on your father?" Makhan asked dubiously.

"May my father die if I am not telling the truth. Look, I'm putting it on my hands, too."

The two friends quietly applied the tallow to their palms during the first four periods and all through the recess hour. Neelkanth's class was after recess. As soon as he entered the classroom, he took off his turban and placed it on the broken shelf of a cupboard. Then he sat down in his chair, unbuttoned his coat and shirt, and began scratching his hairy chest. He stretched his legs, farted and asked the boys to recite their multiplication tables. Makhan was sixth in turn. He did all right through to the three times table, but then he faltered. Neelkanth hauled him forward by his ears. Makhan looked furtively at his hands. They were shining with sheep tallow like a bagel. But Neelkanth did not plan to cane his hands. He surveyed the classroom and noticed that Sulleh was the sturdiest of all the boys.

"Hey, you, Sulleh fatso, come here and lift this snotty fellow onto your back." Sulleh had been quietly referring to his book to memorize the tables. He closed it quickly, shoved it into the cloth bag in which he carried his books, and stood up. He glanced at Makhan, sniggered, and lifted him onto his back. Neelkanth pulled down Makhan's pants and began hitting the soft, tender flesh with his cane.

Makhan screamed, "Oh father dear! Oh mother mine! I am dead. Sir, I swear I'll know them by heart tomorrow! Oh father, I am dead. May God give all your misfortunes to me, Master Ji, tomorrow I will memorize everything, you will see, sir."

"Do you promise?" Neelkanth asked.

"I promise. If I don't know them tomorrow, skin me alive, sir."

"Put him down, then," Neelkanth said to Sulleh before asking the entire class, "Will all of you have learnt the tables till sixteen tomorrow?

"Yes sir," all boys shouted together, Sulleh the loudest of all.

"All those who hadn't learnt the tables for today, pinch your ears in shame."

Several boys pinched their ears, Makhan before everyone else.

At four o'clock, the two friends left for home together. On the way, as Sulleh began to say something, Makhan snapped, "Shut up, you bugger, I know what a loyal friend you are."

"Hey, I didn't put you on my back because I wanted to. I did what Master Ji asked me to do."

"To hell with your sheep tallow!"

"As if I knew he would beat your arse. You should have rubbed it there, it wouldn't have hurt."

"Shut your mouth or I will break your teeth!"

"You are asking for trouble, you lentil-eating Brahmin!"

"Shut up, you gasbag."

When they reached the main road, the convent school bus had just arrived. Children wearing white shirts, red ties, red socks, black shoes and green shorts or skirts, were getting off the bus as their mothers waited for them. They all carried little lunchboxes in their hands. While Sulleh looked at a boy with soft hair and milk-white legs, Makhan fixed his gaze on a girl with blue eyes.

Apparently, the boy had not eaten his lunch, for his mother was saying, "You should have told me that you don't like *keema*, I would have given you some mutton, or a couple of eggs. There were some pieces of fish leftover from yesterday – you could have had those too. Why did you starve yourself?" The boy simply smiled in reply.

Suddenly Sulleh turned to Makhan and asked, "What did they cook at your house today?"

"Collard greens and mallow leaves."

"As plain and boring as I thought."

Makhan did not hear him. Perhaps he was thinking about the blue-eyed girl.

The next day, after the bell had rung, when all the boys had assembled in the school compound for morning prayer, Sulleh happened to look around. He turned deathly pale when he saw his father talking to the headmaster outside the school gate. He thought of running out, but the peon was guarding the gate. The lump of sheep tallow was in his pocket – he had not yet rubbed it on his hands. Soon, the headmaster returned and the peon shut the gate.

"Sulleh of Class IV, step out," commanded the headmaster as he walked in.

Sulleh's legs were trembling, but slowly, he managed to step out of the line. He blew on his hands to warm them.

Waving his cane, the headmaster said, "Do you know what Sulleh did at home yesterday?"

"No, sir," the boys shouted at the top of their voices.

"He threw pots and pans around, smashed drinking glasses and bit his mother's thumb. And do you know why?"

"No, sir."

"He demanded hot rice and a tasty curry."

"Hot rice and tasty curry! Ha ha ha . . ." all the boys laughed.

"Should he have asked for this food?"

"No, sir."

"If your parents give you cold rice, you eat it. If they give you collard greens, you eat them. And if they give you nothing, you stay quiet, right?"

"Yes, sir."

The headmaster hit Sulleh a dozen times on each hand with his cane, and then asked the Molvi Sahib to bite the boy's left thumb. Sulleh bore the sting of the cane on his hands, but the bite made him scream and he slumped to the ground. The headmaster kicked him hard twice, and sent him back to his place among the row of boys.

The morning prayer began. Two boys from Class V – Javed Ahmed and Ashok Kumar – stepped forward and starting singing:

> *My desire comes to my lips as a prayer*
> *O God may my life shine like a candle*

The other boys repeated the lines as loudly as they could. Sulleh, still hiccupping from his sobs, sang through his tears.

> *May my presence rid the world of darkness*
> *May every place brighten with my sparkling light*

After prayer, the boys went to their respective classrooms. When Makhan saw Sulleh, his eyes red and sunken, he was filled with pity and his anger from the previous day vanished. It occurred to him that if his own father had been alive, he too would have come to the school to have him thrashed every now and then. Just as well he was dead. Whatever his mother did to him, she did herself. She would never come to school with a complaint. But the very next moment, he thought of Master Neelkanth and remembered that he had still not memorized his multiplication tables. To ask Sulleh for the sheep tallow now would be awkward. Besides, he had no faith in it anymore. He considered the matter, and in the end, decided that his own remedy seemed to be the best: he muttered Goddess Kali's name seven times and tied a knot in the hem of his shirt.

Neelkanth entered the classroom after recess. As usual, he took off his turban and placed it in the broken cupboard, took his shoes off and sat cross-legged on his chair. As he scratched his head, he asked the students to recite their tables. The first boy had not quite finished when Makhan stood up suddenly.

"And what thunderbolt has hit you, may I ask?"

"I want to go to the toilet."

"Oh, really? Sit down at once or I'll thrash you."

Makhan sat down but stood up again after a few minutes.

"Master Ji, I'm bursting."

"No mischief in my class. I will beat it out of your bottom."

"Master Ji, I'm not lying, I really need to go."

Neelkanth looked at Makhan's face. His eyes were filling with tears. Neelkanth saw that the boy was telling the truth and allowed him to leave.

In the toilet, Makhan began to think that tying a knot at the hem of a shirt really did have power. Otherwise, why had he suddenly felt the urge to shit? He had relieved himself at home in the morning. It's clear, Maha Kali does not abandon her devotees in their hour of need. By the time he got back to the classroom, Neelkanth's class would be done.

School ended at four o'clock, and Makhan and Sulleh set off for home. Sulleh wanted to continue walking when they reached the main road, but Makhan stopped him, "Let's wait for the convent school bus."

"To hell with that. We'll only get beaten for it."

Makhan did not understand what that meant, but he kept quiet. Sulleh took Makhan's arm and tried to pull him along, but Makhan's feet refused to move. Eventually, Sulleh went on alone. But after a short distance, he saw some men playing cards and stopped to watch the game.

A few minutes later, the convent bus arrived and the children dressed in skirts and shorts, socks, shoes and ties, trotted out. The girl with the blue eyes emerged after a few children had got off the bus. She handed her lunchbox and school bag to her mother and tightened the belt on her skirt. Makhan's heart pounded against his ribs, as if the headmaster had made him run around the school compound eight times. He watched her enter the baker's lane.

The next day, school continued as usual until recess when suddenly there was a commotion – two boys had drowned at Habba Kadal. The school bell did not ring for a long time, and when it did, teachers assembled all the boys in the compound and instructed them to stand in rows as they did for morning prayers. After a while, the headmaster came out and delivered a lecture: "Boys must not go to the river ghats to bathe because the river is infested with crocodiles. Crocodile is an aquatic animal that resembles a lizard but it is much bigger in size. As soon as anyone enters the river, its jaws close on his legs and he is dragged down. It's called 'crocodile' in English and 'crocodile tears' is a phrase . . ."

The deputy headmaster came around with a stamp and ink pad to mark every boy's thigh with the school emblem. The headmaster continued his speech: "The stamp of the school is being put on each boy's thigh and we shall check it every day. If this stamp is found erased, the boy will be thrashed with stinging nettles."

As soon as the deputy headmaster had finished stamping all the boys, school was closed for the day.

On the way home, Makhan said to Sulleh, "Suppose we told them we bathed under a tap – how could they tell?"

"Do you think they are fools? They know there's no water in the taps. No chance that your trick will work!"

Makhan pulled up his shorts and said to Sulleh, "See, how beautiful this mark of slavery looks on our thighs."

"Legs of mutton are stamped like this at butcher shops," Sulleh replied.

They reached the main road. Makhan said to Sulleh, "We were spared Neelkanth the Crocodile's class today."

"Yes."

"Did he ask you to recite the tables yesterday?"

"No, I got away, luckily."

"Swear on your father?"

"On my father's death, I swear."

"But how?"

"He asked me to massage his head instead."

They were quiet for a while, and then Makhan said, "The convent bus hasn't come today."

"It can't come now, we were let off early today. Let's go."

"Let's wait."

"No, the Crocodile is sure to demand his tables tomorrow."

But Makhan had developed faith in the power of a knot in the hem of his shirt. So he replied indifferently, "We will see, tomorrow is a long way off."

Tomorrow came and went for many days, for what seemed like a long time. The form master was made responsible for the boys' hygiene, and before the morning prayer, he would ask them to show him the stamps on their thighs. The stamp had faded completely for many of the boys but some still had a faint impression on their thighs. However, Sulleh's and Makhan's were as fresh as if they were new. In fact, the layers of grime that had accumulated around the impressions made them more visible. The form master understood that this pair had obeyed the headmaster's order to the letter while the others had surreptitiously taken an occasional bath. He was pleased with the two. Letting them off early, he sent them to work with the carpenters at his own house.

Sulleh and Makhan were happy to be working at the form master's house. Their job was to pass the planks, beams, and nails to the carpenters, fill water in the hookah, tamp tobacco in its bowl, place the embers carefully, and puff at it till it was properly lit. The beams tore Makhan's shirt. Sulleh was smarter . . . he had taken off his shirt and worked in only his shorts.

At four o'clock, the boys picked up their bundles of books and left for home. As they reached the main road, Makhan's feet automatically came to a halt. Sulleh laughed and stopped too. Soon, the Convent school bus arrived and the children started to alight. Today, they wore their winter uniforms – black shoes, red socks, warm grey flannel pants and sweaters, white shirts, red ties, and cherry-red blazers with school badges pinned on the upper pockets. Makhan looked hard, but could not see the girl with the blue eyes. "Let's go . . . it's getting late and it's cold," Sulleh's words jolted Makhan out of his thoughts. He felt the cold too, and they headed home.

About a month later, school closed for the winter vacation. When it reopened, there was still snow on roads, boundary walls, and in yards. The boys had snowball fights before the school bell rang. Sulleh and Makhan buried many boys in the snow, thrust snowballs down the collars of many others, and made snow effigies of the headmaster, Master Neelkanth, and Molvi Sahib. In their excitement, they realized for the first time how good they were at these games. They spared hardly anyone. Dragging Ashok Kumar and Javed Ahmed of Class V through the snow doubled their glee, and this game lasted until the fourth period. No teacher showed up in class for the first two periods. The third period was Molvi Sahib's. He demanded Shivaratri walnuts from the Pandit students and forgot to check the homework assigned for the vacation. But in the fourth period, the deputy headmaster entered the classroom and demanded the homework immediately. Many boys turned deathly pale. Makhan quickly tied a knot in the hem of his shirt. Sulleh did not seem to have the lump of tallow with him. He looked up at the deputy headmaster with a beseeching expression in his eyes. The deputy headmaster asked Sulleh, Makhan and all the others who had not done their homework to stand up. He banged on the wood stove's pipes with a stick, collected the fallen soot and smeared it on their faces. He ordered the class monitor to parade them around all the classrooms. Makhan heaved a sigh of relief at having escaped a beating. He was now totally convinced that tying a knot in the hem of the shirt had divine powers. As he went down the stairs, he said to Sulleh, "The other day, on Shivaratri, I watched a film with my cousin. The black giant in it looked exactly like you."

"You should see your own face, you look like a monster", Sulleh retorted.

The class monitor took them first to Class V, where the teacher and the students laughed at them; the boys joined in with stupid smiles on their faces. Then he took them to Class III, which at that moment was being taught by Master Neelkanth, who pulled their ears. A few students started to laugh, but Sulleh gave them such a malevolent look that the laughter froze on their lips. Then, the monitor took them to Class II, which was being taught by Molvi Sahib.

He slapped a few of the boys and shouted obscenities at some of the others. He slapped Makhan on the back and warned him, "Don't you dare forget to bring me Shivaratri walnuts tomorrow."

In the Upper 1st, Makhan quietly pinched Sulleh, the black devil in front of him, who shrieked, earning him a few lashes from the teacher there. In Lower 1st, Sulleh kicked the inkpots of the students sitting in the first row, but they were too scared to even whimper. When the boys got back to their classroom, the deputy headmaster instructed them to squat with their arms looped around their knees and hold their ears as he barked at them to bring their finished homework the next day without fail.

Tomorrow came and went for the next five years. The name of the school changed to Government Lower Middle School, but it still had the same five classes and Sulleh and Makhan remained in Class IV. The mellow autumn sunshine was pleasant and Molvi Sahib put the two boys to work. Sulleh was scratching the teacher's back and haunches with his nails. Makhan was popping the boils on his thighs. Molvi Sahib's eyes were slits of pleasure. Other boys played tic-tac-toe on their slates, and the monitor stood at the door on the lookout for the headmaster.

Molvi Sahib's was the last class of the day. Makhan bought a cigarette from the shop outside the school for one paisa and both friends took turns puffing at it.

"C'mon! Let's dump our books at home and play in the dungyard," Sulleh said to Makhan.

"Let's finish the cigarette first. Someone might see us smoking on the main road."

"Stop lying, bugger. If your father were alive, you would have made him pack your pipe with tobacco. I know what's going through your mind. She's not going to come this early."

Makhan grinned.

By the time they finished their cigarette and got to the main road, the convent bus had already arrived. The children got down and went off with their mothers. The bus left, but Makhan and Sulleh stayed. Makhan got Sulleh to buy roasted soybeans for two *paise* and they began tossing the beans into their mouths.

"There she comes," Makhan forgot to chew the soybeans in his mouth when he heard Sulleh's comment. His heart raced, and he stared at the girl, wide-eyed.

She got off her bicycle near the baker's lane. Her school bag was in the bicycle's carrier and she held a hockey stick in her right hand. She was wearing white sneakers and white socks. Her white skirt was slightly above her knees, a red cardigan was tied around her white shirt. Her hair was shoulder-length.

"Well, she's grown up, hasn't she? And changed a lot."

"Only her blue eyes are the same," Makhan sighed deeply.

"She used to be such a little girl!"

"As little as we were! Apparently, she's appearing for matriculation exams this year."

"Swear on your father's life?" Sulleh was startled.

"Yes."

"What luck!"

"They say she is also the captain of her school hockey team."

Suddenly, Sulleh remembered something. He asked Makhan, "Didn't they take four *annas* from each of us at school for sports equipment last month . . . what did they do with that money?" Makhan was annoyed by this digression. How like a Muslim to go off on a tangent, he thought.

After twelve years, the name of the school was changed again, this time to Nehru Memorial Government Lower Middle School.

"What does this Nehru Memorial mean?" Sulleh asked Makhan.

"Nehru Ji died recently, that's why they've named our school after him," he replied.

"I know that, but what does 'memorial' mean?"

"How the hell should I know?"

"It sounds like an obscenity to me."

"What the hell is wrong with you?" Makhan lost his cool. "I'll tell Headmaster Sahib that you're being disrespectful to the leader of the Kashmiri Pandits."

"I didn't start it! They're the ones who chose to rename the school."

"Why the hell does it concern you? Just keep your mouth shut."

That day after the morning prayer, the headmaster announced that Molvi Sahib was retiring with immediate effect and would no longer be coming to school. He spoke at length of Molvi Sahib's virtues and talents, but the boys did not recognize the person he described. Then he requested that Molvi Sahib speak to the boys and counsel them. Molvi Sahib stepped forward and began to speak, but broke down after just a few words. He took a handkerchief out of his *achkan* pocket and wiped his tears. He brought the same kerchief to his nose and blew hard into it, folded it carefully around the snot it had collected, and put it back in his pocket.

As they climbed the stairs to the classroom, Makhan asked Sulleh, "Why did Molvi Sahib cry?"

"Well, he would! His job's gone."

"Maybe he was feeling sorry for beating us so much?"

"Maybe, who knows."

"Anyway, good riddance. God has saved us from him."

"You think the one who replaces him will be any better? These buggers are all alike."

That day, Molvi Sahib went to Class IV as usual, for his teaching period. Squawking like a parrot, he said, "My dear boys, you'll be happy to see me gone. You must resent me a lot because I used to beat you. But remember, a teacher's beating is not really a beating, it is like sustenance. This cane is not just a cane, it grants wisdom. I held no grudge against anyone, rather my heart was filled with affection for you, and that's why I used this cane of wisdom to teach you something."

The boys listened to Molvi Sahib in silence. He prattled on for a while, and finally, he said, "Today, for the last time, I shall hit each of you once with this cane so that you will remember my affection for you forever."

Molvi Sahib retired but nobody replaced him for a while. The following day, the headmaster himself took the class. When he saw Sulleh in the classroom, he seemed to remember something important.

"What is your name?" he asked.

"Sulleh, sir."

"Alright, Sulleh, get up and go to my house . . . do you know where I live?"

"Yes, sir."

"Good. Our servant went to his village yesterday. Take our cow out to graze."

Sulleh stood up quickly. "Sir, shall I leave my books here or take them along?"

"No, take the books with you. You can go directly home at 4 o'clock. But you should take another person with you."

"I can take Makhan with me, sir."

"Who is Makhan?"

"Me, sir," Makhan got up with a grin.

"Alright. On the double!"

The boys picked up their books and left quickly. They went to Headmaster Sahib's house and took the cow out to a distant pasture. The cow grazed, and the two boys played hopscotch.

"Did you see how fat the headmaster's wife is?" Makhan said to Sulleh.

"Of course she'd be fat! With a cow at home . . . she must drink milk by the bucketful every day."

"She said the servant would be back in four days. As if we care, these four days are well set up for us."

"And if we have to write an essay on a cow in the exams, just think of it," Sulleh said.

"Look, this cow indeed has two ears, two eyes, four legs and a tail. Don't they also say 'a cow chews the cud' – what does that mean?"

"You know cows produce dung. Perhaps cow dung is called 'chewing the cud' in Urdu." Sulleh replied after giving the matter some thought.

"Anyway, if the headmaster is pleased with us, he will definitely pass us, essay or no essay," said Makhan.

"I'll bring marbles tomorrow . . . hopscotch isn't that fun."

"Good plan!" Makhan jumped with joy.

On the fourth day, while playing marbles, Makhan suddenly heaved a deep sigh and said, "The headmaster's wife said that their servant will be back from his village today."

"That means we have to go to school tomorrow," Sulleh's heart sank.

"Yes, no choice."

"Let's wander around tomorrow as well. We can tell people at home that we have to take headmaster's cow to the pasture."

"On my father's life, you have truly uttered words of wisdom!" Makhan exclaimed and made his next move.

Tomorrow came and went for another five years. It was the 14th of November, Jawaharlal Nehru's birthday, which was celebrated as Children's Day. In the morning, Sulleh, Makhan and other boys of the

Nehru Memorial Lower Middle School were taken to the city stadium by their teachers. The massive stadium gate was decorated with arches and paper garlands. A number of cars were parked on either side of the road, which was sprinkled with water and lined with lime. Policemen in freshly laundered and ironed uniforms patrolled the area.

The boys of the Nehru Memorial Government Lower Middle School were not allowed to enter from the front gate. They were ushered in from the back of the stadium. Sulleh and Makhan were amazed at what they saw inside. Red, blue, yellow, green, pink and purple flags danced in the wind. Men in expensive suits and women in colourful saris sat on one side. Boys from different schools in distinct and attractive uniforms stood in front of them. On the other side, a band dazzled in its ceremonial attire, as its drums and bugles glittered in the sun.

Sulleh, Makhan and several other boys were made to sit in a remote corner at the back, away from all the activity. They tried to push their way to the front unobtrusively, but were caught by a teacher who waved his mulberry cane and drove them back. Makhan would rise up on his toes every now and then in order to catch a glimpse of the show, but Sulleh was happily engaged in a game of pebbles with another boy.

Suddenly, people stood up from their chairs. Someone said something through the megaphone and the uniformed boys rose to attention. A man dressed in snow-white clothes with a smile on his face arrived and greeted everyone with folded hands. He sat down on a sofa in the front row.

Sulleh gently tossed a pebble at Makhan.

"Which bugger's father died"? Makhan responded angrily.

"Nobody's, I threw it." Sulleh explained. "Tell me, who's that guy?"

"Who knows? Somebody important, I guess."

"Is he the one who will give us the pears?"

"Who told you they're going to distribute pears here?"

"Neelkanth told us earlier that we'll get two pears each."

"Swear on your father's life?" Makhan was pleased.

"Yes, on my father's life."

The man in white went to the dais and hoisted the national flag. Everyone stood up, the boys saluted and the band performed. People sat back in their chairs and the man began to speak.

"What is he saying?" Makhan asked Sulleh.

"I can't understand a thing," he replied.

The man finished speaking and returned to his seat. People clapped. Sulleh, Makhan and other boys also clapped loudly. After this, a little girl went on to the stage and sang a song; she too was cheered by the audience, and Makhan and Sulleh clapped along. Then a few boys went on stage and said something, and they also received loud applause.

"I am tired of this clapping," Sulleh said to Makhan.

"You get tired very quickly," Makhan retorted. "These poor people didn't get tired making speeches but you got tired of clapping!"

A group of girls performed a traditional dance, which was followed by a drill display by the boys in uniform. At the end of it, the man-in-white ascended the dais again and gave away prizes to the boys and girls. Each winner was cheered by the crowd.

"When will they give us the pears?" Sulleh asked Makhan.

"How should I know? They may not," replied Makhan.

"Why not? If they can give prizes to those people, why would they not give us something too?"

"You think only of your stomach. As if you're starving."

"I swear, I've eaten nothing all morning."

"Didn't you even drink tea?"

"It wasn't ready when I left home."

"Oh . . . Okay, hush! Look, another woman's got a prize, clap for her."

"Right now!" Sulleh said and clapped loudly. "I could die for her."

The show finally ended at eleven o'clock. Sulleh and Makhan walked out and stood at the stadium gate. Munching on their pears, the two friends counted the cars and jeeps that drove by.

"Forty-seven."

"Forty-eight."

"Forty-nine."

"Fifty."

"Fifty-one."

"Hell with them. What's the point of this . . . it will only tire us out."

"I didn't realize there were so many cars and jeeps in the city."

"This is nothing, there are actually four times as many!"

"Really! Swear on your father's life?"

"On my father's life. To hell with them. You said they would give us two pears, why did they give us only one?"

"How should I know? Maybe the teachers took half the pears home."

"Did you see who was in that car?" Makhan was almost shouting.

"No. Who?" Sulleh asked.

"That girl with the blue eyes. Maybe she has her daughter in the car with her."

"Was her husband with her?" Sulleh asked.

"Yes."

"The boy who used to have silky hair and milk-white legs." Sulleh sighed.

"Yes, that one."

"Have they grown older?"

"Of course they have!"

"I bet they have children too."

"Obviously! Twenty-two or twenty-three years must have passed."

"Twenty-two or twenty-three years!"

"Yes! It was a lifetime ago."

"Yes!"

"True. Nehru Ji had just begun to rule the country at that time. Now his daughter is in power."

"Swear on your father's life?"

"Yes, on my father's life."

"Why didn't we grow up?"

"I don't know. They say fools don't grow up."

"Then wretches probably don't grow up either, right?"

"I don't know. Can't say."

"Do we have to go to school tomorrow?" Makhan asked after a while.

"Don't you want to go? They gave you a holiday today – you expect one more tomorrow?"

"I wondered if they might."

"They didn't even give us two pears."

"I guess we have to go to school tomorrow", Makhan sighed.

The next day, after the morning assembly, when the boys began to enter their classrooms, Sulleh of Class IV said to Makhan, "Learnt the tables for Neelkanth, bugger?"

"No. You?"

"Tried, but couldn't memorize them."

"What do we do now? He is a real pain in the neck." Makhan's face grew pale.

Sulleh laughed it off and quietly slipped something to Makhan. "Here, rub this on your hands, bugger."

"What is it?"

"Sheep tallow. Rub it on your hands and the caning won't hurt."

"Swear on your father?" Makhan asked dubiously.

"May my father die if I am not telling the truth. Look, I am putting it on my hands too.

Curfew

HE LIT HIS CIGARETTE BUT HAD MANAGED TO TAKE ONLY A couple of drags before he heard the door of the other room open. He hurriedly stubbed the cigarette out against the wall and began picking his nose like an innocent child. But Băb did not enter his room. He went straight downstairs instead.

"Messing up my routine again!" he muttered in annoyance. He lit the cigarette once more. As he smoked by the window that opened on to the compound, his mind drifted. He saw Băb sitting on the big stone mortar talking to Ram Joo from the Tikkoo family. Băb did not have his usual turban on. He ran his hand over his forehead while deep in conversation. He had worn a turban all his life and the impression that this had formed on his forehead was visible from the room above. Băb's face was not too dark. But the part of his forehead that remained covered by the turban was considerably fairer than the rest. This fairer skin framed a darker triangular shape. He was surprised that he had started noticing this triangle only recently. It was Băb's daily shaves that had probably given him blemishes between his chin and his lower lip, he speculated. He hadn't noticed these before, either. It was as though he had begun to see his father in a new light: perhaps the true self that he had been unable to perceive earlier. He may never have had the chance to observe his father so closely had it not been for the curfew.

The curfew had provided him with a fresh perspective that not only familiarized him with the triangular shape on Băb's forehead and the blemishes on his chin, but also with the crookedness of the walls of his own room. A few months before, he had redone the windows of the room and painted its walls. He had also bought a couple of chairs and a teapoy from the market. Apart from his books, he had placed a radio, a table lamp, a clock, an electric kettle, a toaster and decorative objects on the shelves. He was pleased with himself after he had arranged these things and believed that from now on he could lead a more modern life in that old room. But since he had been in the same room without a break for the last few days, he began to reassess its decor and to feel ashamed of it. The paint, layered upon mud plaster, had already developed cracks, giving the walls the texture of diseased skin. The leaky wooden ceiling had developed mold in some places. The new windows did not match the old frames and arranging modern objects and bric-a-brac on crooked shelves, originally meant for old-fashioned vessels, now seemed like a stupid idea.

Băb and Ram Joo were talking about the good old times and their despair with the current situation. They mentioned the recent tragedies in muted tones. They avoided saying too much and resorted to gestures every now and then in order to express themselves fully. "They say they had a program . . ." said Băb and then was silent as he gestured with his right hand as if wielding a knife through the air. He felt like shouting from his window: "Hey Pandit Sahib, where do you get these ideas from? You've been peeing indoors in a clay pot all these days! Go back to your prayer room and recite Ram! Ram!" He moved from that window and sat by the other one that looked out onto the street. A part of the road was visible from there. Earlier, the road had been deserted, with only a few military men patrolling it every now and then. But now several people, returning from Ameera Kadal, walked by carrying plastic bags filled with peas, cauliflower, tomatoes, Surf detergent, and Dalda tins. He sighed. If he'd been employed, he too would have had a curfew pass. He too could have gone to Ameera Kadal, sat in Coffee House, or watched a film in a cinema hall. Perhaps the news reports about normalcy prevailing in the town are true, he thought. Had the situation not been normal, people wouldn't need passes to be on the roads, go to their offices, or wander around in Ameera Kadal and buy delightful groceries from the market. The administrators must have issued a lot of passes this time, he thought. But for those who have passes there is no disorder or curfew anywhere in the town! Curfews affect only those who are killed with bullets, or are struck with batons or slashed with knives. Only the ones whose houses are set on fire know how it feels. Curfews are selective; imposed on some and not others

After taking a few more puffs, he threw the cigarette butt out onto the street and moved away from the window. He wrapped himself in a bed sheet and lay down. He tried to sleep but could not catch even a wink. Finally, he got up, folded the sheet and switched on the radio. A film song was playing. He liked the song. It was followed by another. This one was good too. Perhaps the radio station is deliberately playing good songs to pacify those who don't have curfew passes, he thought.

He was still listening to the second song when Băb came upstairs and walked into his room. His heart sank. He got up quickly and switched off the radio. Băb sat in a chair right across from him. He began to re-examine the contours of the triangular shape on his father's forehead.

"Listening to film songs, were you?" Băb said with a snigger. "It's these film songs that have led to all this trouble! There's no sense of shame anymore! Things were not so vulgar in our times. If we felt like listening to music, we would listen to religious music! These days neither Hindus nor Muslims care about religion. It's a wonder we're not struck by thunderbolts from the skies!"

He felt suffocated. "Why is he going on and on like a runaway train?" He felt like telling him, you'd only be happy if I wasted hours in the prayer room every morning just like you do! You don't find me religious enough, but how religious are you? The whole neighborhood knows it all too well! On the one hand you keep ringing bells for the gods. On the other, you are leering at Baggĕ Lala's Kamlawati!

"How long before the news comes on?" Băb asked. He looked at his watch and said, "Still about seven or eight minutes." But even as he was saying this, he regretted it, knowing that now Băb would continue to sit in front of him for all that time. He should have lied and said the next news bulletin was more than half an hour away. Băb wouldn't wait that long and would have gone back to his room. These days he seemed to be totally obsessed with the news! If the news is read on the radio ten times a day, he comes to my room twenty times . . .

"Listen! Perhaps they will lift the curfew for an hour tomorrow as well."

He realized this was just an opening! Băb was about to say something that he wouldn't want to hear. He felt a strange restlessness, as though he were sitting on thorns.

"Early tomorrow morning you should go to Wostĕ Mohammad's house and make all the arrangements with him so that he can start work as soon as the curfew is lifted." Băb took a match stick out of the box and started cleaning his ear.

"The whole wall will collapse if this pillar is not repaired soon." He listened to him without paying too much attention. Let's assume we repair this wall today, what guarantee is there that the other wall will not collapse tomorrow? he thought. Why doesn't Băb realize that this whole house is on the verge of collapsing? A day earlier or a day later, it is still bound to crumble. But Băb thinks highly of his seven-columned, three-storied house. More than half of it is filled with old pots, rusted tin shards, and ragged quilts from his great-grandfather's time. Maybe it had been grand once, but now, with all the beautiful new houses that had come up around it, its great length and breadth were a matter of embarrassment.

"Today the problem can be fixed with a hundred rupees, tomorrow the same repairs will cost a thousand."

He understood which hundred rupees his father had in mind. He had tried to hide the fact that he had got a third student to tutor, but Băb had heard about it from somewhere. He would keep forty rupees from each of the other two tuitions for himself. A hundred and twenty went toward household expenses. He had thought to keep the additional hundred for his own use, but now it seemed Băb already had other plans.

"So, what have you thought?"

"The new tuition folks have not paid me yet!" he panicked as though someone had caught him stealing.

"They'll pay you, eventually," said Băb. "Tell me, will you go to see Wostĕ Mohammad, or should I go myself?"

"No, I will!" he thought it better to put an end to this conversation.

"Times have changed. You have no idea! When I had the roof redone, Wostĕ Mohammad's father did not charge me a penny. He needed my help for some official paperwork!"

He stared as his father. When had Băb been employed by the government? How long ago would Wostĕ Mohammad's father's papers have been in his charge? His father had lived on a pension ever since he could remember. As far as he was concerned, Băb had been retired longer than he had worked.

Băb said nothing but stood by quietly, waiting for the news broadcast. He looked at his watch. There were still four minutes for the news to start. Having to sit with his father for another four minutes would be torture. He got up and stood next to the window looking onto the street with his back to Băb. He happened to see Usha from the Razdan house. Usha, who was trying on a tight shalwar-kameez, was admiring herself in the mirror. He kept the window half open and watched her stealthily. Usha was probably trying on this outfit for the first time. He guessed it must have been bought by her father, brother, or uncle, one of whom must have just fetched it for her from the tailor on the Bund or in Lambert Lane. Even the servants in that house had curfew passes! Usha's father appeared to do nothing, and yet, he is a wealthy man, spending time with important people.

Usha looked particularly good in her henna-colored outfit. The shalwar was rather bright and clearly made of synthetic material. The tunic was a slightly lighter shade, and its sheen suggested that it must be made of Terylene or Terysilk. She turned her left profile towards the mirror and stretched slightly which accentuated her small crabapple-like breasts. She twisted her neck around to look at her buttocks. Noticing her firm behind and her delicate waist made his heart beat faster.

She pulled a shawl from her cupboard and arranged it over her shoulders and breasts. She drew one end of it over her head in the manner of a bride. Then she tied it like a turban on her head, like a gangster, and started winking and whistling at her reflection in the mirror. And then . . .

"Come on! Switch on the radio now! It must be time!"

He swallowed his anger and switched on the radio, even though he actually wanted to throw it at his father's head.

The news began. The first item was about the likelihood of a good autumn crop across the state; the second was about Vietnam; the third on developments in West Asia; the fourth on improving international tourism in the country; the fifth about a plane crash somewhere in the Americas. That was all. There was no mention of what Băb so desperately wanted to hear. Băb looked downcast, and this pleased his son. Băb continued to sit in the room even though the news bulletin was over. He was getting really anxious now. Usually, he met Băb only once every few days, over dinner. But these last few days he had had to see his father's face from morning to evening, and that on an empty stomach!

"What is this? The radio did not even mention the curfew?"

He kept silent.

"We have been imprisoned for no reason."

True, we have been imprisoned, he felt like saying, but that is not so painful. The real torment is that the two of us have been locked up in the same cell!

There was noise from the corridor below and then the sound of Tosha crying. He guessed that his mother and his aunt had been bickering again – with his aunt lamenting, as usual, for her dead husband, and his mother thrashing Tosha for no reason other than to assuage her anger.

We have to put up with this widow aunt, on top of everything else! He thought of her two daughters who were both well-to-do. But she would not stay with them. In her view, to be dependent on daughters for food was tantamount to eating cow dung. That's why she had turned up in our house to eat pulao!

Băb's anger was evident in his reddening earlobes. He got up abruptly and left the moment he heard Aunt wailing, shutting the door hard. The ill-fitting door moaned like a dying person. He knew that Băb would now make his mother the target of his rage. The poor fellow has lost his mind. The walls and the ceiling of the corridor have become dark with smoke. The floor is damp due to seepage. These women sit on a couple of damp reed mats all day. Why wouldn't they quarrel, squabble and snarl at each other? We can't expect them to sing, can we?

He sat down by the window again. He looked across at the Razdan house but the room was empty now. Usha had folded her henna-colored outfit, placed it on a table, and gone somewhere. He looked up at the tower of the house and then at the garden, but she was nowhere to be seen. He heard the whistle of the pressure cooker from their kitchen, and the aroma of yakhni reached his window. He presumed that even under these circumstances, the Razdans were entertaining at least three or four guests. I wonder what delicacies are being prepared! Usha will serve her guests in her new henna-colored clothes. The guests will leave the house after dinner at about eleven. Then their servant will, as usual, place the leftovers and bones near my window. The dogs will come from all over and fight for the food. They will raise hell and not let me sleep a wink. He was already worried. He opened the window as far as it would go and looked out at the street.

The street was livelier than before. Băb had been worried for no reason! Why would the radio mention a curfew when there was none! Everything is normal. People with passes are moving about with no fear. There is no curfew in Ameera Kadal. Shops must be open; hotels and restaurants full; movies showing in the cinemas . . . and Ameera Kadal is just three or four hundred meters from here.

As he was thinking about all this, he saw three strangers walking along and laughing loudly. Their laughter pulled at his heart. He felt strangely suffocated. He felt like going out on the street and shouting: What is my fault? Give me a pass as well. Give me a job too. It's been two years since I completed my master's degree. If Băb extracted free work from Wostĕ Mohammad's father by holding his papers to ransom, why should I have to pay the price? Is it my fault that Băb is my father? I have no sympathy for him. I hate him!

He felt exhausted, as though he had actually shouted slogans on the street; hurled stones at the military; as if he had burnt a few buses and a few trucks; as if he had pulled out electric wires and telephone cables – he got up from the window and lay down, resting his head on his elbows. He tried hard to fall asleep but failed. Suddenly he remembered something. He got up and flung open his brief case.

He pulled out his wallet and drew out ten notes of ten rupees each. He counted them, put them back in the wallet and the wallet back in the brief case. One hundred rupees, he thought. A lot can be bought with this amount. I can go to Pahalgam or Gulmarg and stay there for five or six days in some hotel or cottage. I can get a pair of henna-colored Terylene trousers tailored. I can even buy a pressure cooker with this sum. Or, I can take this money and leave this place altogether. Go away from this house, far away from this city and do whatever I like. Giving this amount to Băb for repairs is a waste. This house has to collapse one day or the other, in a month or six months or a year or six . . . Or maybe things would take an untoward turn tonight and become as bad as they were the day before the curfew. Or maybe they would get worse and some courageous youth would set the whole neighborhood on fire, including this house.

It's possible that someone would set this house on fire tonight. He felt a strange sense of joy imagining this, a sense of great relief . . . and using his elbows as a pillow, he lay down again and began to feel sleepy.

One Sahib and the Other

THE TEA ARRIVED. AS ONE SAHIB STARTED TO POUR THE TEA, he said to the other Sahib, "You have an obstructionist, communal, and obsolete mentality. You want to sell our country. You deceive people. You want to create riots with your inflammatory speeches so that the country does not prosper. But thankfully, people are alert. They understand your tricks very well. Some innocents might still fall for your sweet talk, but God willing, we shall expose you to them as well."

"How many spoons of sugar would you like in your tea?"

"Just one."

"Since when have you cut back on sugar?"

"It's been more than a year," the other Sahib replied.

"The doctor has advised me to consume less sugar, eat chapatti instead of rice for one meal and fast once a week."

"Has it helped?"

"It has, indeed. Don't you think I've lost weight since last year?"

"Yes, you do look better."

The two Sahibs drank their tea without any further conversation. When they had finished, one Sahib lit a cigarette and said to the other, "You are a ruthless dictator. Hitler, Mussolini and Stalin were amateurs in comparison. If someone utters a word against you, they are imprisoned, tortured and their mouth is stuffed with hot potatoes. And as for prosperity – there's none under your rule. People have become poorer. You and your legions of goons have made people destitute. But mind you, nobody, however powerful, stays forever. Least of all you. God willing, we'll get rid of you soon. By the way, how's Baby doing with her painting?"

"She puts together a series of random lines and calls it modern art. I honestly don't understand it."

"Call it modern art or modernism, the concept has plagued literature too. Neither poems nor stories are comprehensible anymore. You can't make any sense of them."

"Thankfully, this idea of modernism hasn't yet entered politics. If it had, we'd no longer understand each other."

Both Sahibs laughed out loud.

At that very moment, someone entered the room and whispered in the first Sahib's ear, who then turned to the other Sahib and said, "You have been asked to join us for lunch."

"Oh no, I cannot. Please, may I be excused?"

"Why? Have lunch. Our disagreements are not personal. It's a clash of principles."

"You're right, absolutely. Ours is a battle of principles, and I can lay down my life for what I believe in. People know this, and that is why they love me. I have pledged to end your tyranny. Our relationship, of course, will remain unaffected as always."

"Did Munna appear for the examination?"

"Yes, he did."

"How did it go?"

"He said it went well. We'll know soon."

"What does he want to do?"

"Whatever's possible."

"What do you feel? If you want, we could send him abroad to study further. Or get him a lucrative job here. Our disagreements are between us; our children are not a part of them. Munna is like my own son."

"Of course."

"Once he passes the exams, send him to me. I'll talk to him."

"Of course."

The first Sahib lit his pipe. After a few puffs, he said to the other Sahib, "I read your editorial the other day. A good piece I have to say."

"Oh yes, I was severely critical of the extremist elements in your party. They're always saying things that have no foundation. Every party has extremists who create trouble."

"We don't agree with your party either, and we'll challenge you soon enough."

"You are free to say what you please."

Both Sahibs were silent for some time – one puffing on his pipe, the other browsing through a book of pictures. Then the first Sahib asked the other, "Have you made up your mind about lunch?"

"Yes, I'd be happy to stay. The invitation has come from your wife, so I accept it. I would never agree if you had asked me. I cannot compromise my principles."

A while later, four men entered the room. The first Sahib shook hands with them and asked them to sit. The second Sahib remained engrossed in his book.

"You must have found out that we're coming to your constituency tomorrow."

"You are wise and experienced workers. I don't need to tell you what to do," the first Sahib replied.

"You will receive a rousing welcome, sir," one of the four said.

"The welcome is not for me but for the cause and the values that are dear to us. I am a mere symbol of these values and that cause."

The men clapped enthusiastically.

The Sahib pulled a bundle of cash out of his coat pocket and handed it over to them.

"Sir, it will be a rousing welcome – gates, decorations, firecrackers, garlands, everything will be high class . . . so splendid that our opponents will be stunned," said another man.

The first Sahib chuckled. The four men then glared at the other Sahib. But he was still wrapped up in his book. He was either oblivious to their conversation or thought it unwise to interfere.

After the four had left, he said to the first Sahib, "So you are scheduled to visit your constituency tomorrow, and they haven't completed the arrangements yet."

"It won't take them long."

"We are already prepared."

"Really? What's your plan?"

"We'll wave black flags at you in three places. That's all."

"Have you made the flags?"

"They must have had them made them by now. I bought the cloth a few days ago."

"Your workers are doing good work in the area."

"They have to. After all, we are fighting for a great cause."

"I am not afraid of all this. The people are with me," the first Sahib declared.

"The people are with us," said the second Sahib, in a louder voice.

For a while, silence reigned. Then the Sahib smoking a cigarette said to the Sahib who was smoking a pipe, "Could you lend me five hundred rupees?"

"What for?"

"I have to pay for the black cloth, and I need some money to distribute to the crowds."

Suddenly there was a loud noise from outside the house. Both Sahibs were startled. The Sahib with the pipe sent someone to find out what had happened. The man returned after a while.

"Sir, your supporters were marching in a procession," he reported to the Sahib with the pipe. "They were shouting slogans in praise of you. They entered the lane and saw a procession of his party approaching from the other end," he pointed to the Sahib with the cigarette.

"Then what happened?" the Sahib with the cigarette asked.

"The usual, sir. Both processions stopped in the lane, each side started shouting their slogans louder and louder. Then a fight broke out. They threw stones at each other. Thirty-one people are reported to have been injured, and eleven of them are in critical condition."

Both Sahibs became solemn. They were quiet for a long time, and then they looked at each other with resignation.

"This is very sad," one Sahib eventually remarked.

"Violence is wrong. It has to be condemned," said the other Sahib. "Political battles are fought on principles. Violence demeans these ideals and wounds them."

"Actually, our people have still not developed a political consciousness," the first Sahib heaved a great sigh. His pipe had gone out. He lit it again with a match.

The second Sahib said nothing. His eyes had welled up. He put out his cigarette and began to wipe his tears with a handkerchief.

For Now, It Is Night

IT WAS SO COLD! I FELT AS IF I WERE SLEEPING ON ICE. IT WAS a large room and there were three of us in it. The windows were shut but they were without panes. Outside, it was raining heavily and the strong winds from the Pir Panjal came in gusts. This wind, this biting cold of Banihal, blew strongly through the room of the tourist hostel. Despite being indoors, it was as if we were sleeping outside.

Our bedclothes were soaked even though they had been covered with a tarpaulin, and so we had had to rent three blankets each from the caretaker of the hostel.

I had used one as a mattress on the cot and wrapped myself in the other two. Makhan had done the same. Swami Ji, who was still not asleep, had arranged two blankets under him like a seat and had one on his knees. He was reading a book.

The cold had entered my bones. My back, shoulders and buttocks were aching badly. I was strangely restless; I tossed and turned. Makhan had curled up and was sleeping close by. I put my hand on his shoulder and said, "Come, let's sleep in each other's arms. It might keep us warm."

He pushed my hand off his shoulder and hid his head under the blanket. He was upset with me, and if I thought about it, his anger was justified. After reaching Banihal, when the driver had announced that we were halting for the night, Makhan had been the only one who had argued. He had insisted that the driver continue through the night to reach a safer place, but it was of no use. If we had supported Makhan, the driver might have relented. But we were silent. Many of us were probably afraid of crossing the Banihal Pass in the dark, particularly when the driver was not willing to do so. Makhan had had a long argument with the driver but had lost in the end. Now he was not as angry with the driver as he was with the other passengers who had not supported him.

I could not sleep. I got up and leaned against the wall. I looked at Swami Ji. He was immersed in his thoughts, with the book open in front of him.

He raised his eyebrows as if to ask what the matter was.

"It's really cold, Swami Ji."

He laughed. "Why do you feel so cold? I don't."

"Why would he feel cold? God has made him plump. Cold can't go through fat," Makhan muttered so that only I could hear. He was more annoyed with Swami Ji than with anyone else, because at Ramban, Swami Ji had got off the bus and disappeared, and that had cost us half an hour. If we had not wasted that half hour, we would have crossed the most dangerous stretch of road before the landslide occurred near Khooni Nala, and we would have been happily home by now. Makhan believed that Swami Ji was the reason for our predicament. However, there could have been another reason, which perhaps hadn't crossed Makhan's mind. It's possible that Swami Ji had a vision about the landslide, and so he had delayed our bus for half an hour at Ramban. If he hadn't, who knows, our bus might have slid down the slope. They say God does everything for a reason.

I pulled both blankets over myself again and tried to sleep but couldn't. The pain in my shoulders and buttocks worsened, and it made me even more restless. On the one hand, the cold had frozen every joint in my body, and on the other, a peculiar dread had settled in my heart. For the first time in my life, I'd seen a mountain collapse. The landslide had occurred near Khooni Nala. A few small rocks fell as we were standing there and talking. We ignored them. But the sight of narrow cracks in the mountain widening right in front of our eyes had frightened us. Then, with a thunderous roar that was terrifying, the entire mountain began to crumble. We screamed and ran, and when we looked back, we saw a part of the mountain sliding down like a waterfall and vanishing from sight. Huge rocks were crushed to pieces and cypress trees tumbled down with the mud and stones. Watching this instilled a strange fear in my heart which I have yet to overcome.

The road opened for traffic after six hours, but an incessant rain began that intensified as time passed.

I turned in my bed, drew my knees close to my chest, and placed my hands between them. The rain hammered down on the rocks outside, and the biting cold entered the hostel room from one end and exited from the other. I realized that the passengers who had stayed back in the bus had been wiser.

Suddenly, the electricity went off and I panicked. Now, what gripped me was terror. I slowly rose to my feet and approached Swami Ji.

"Swami Ji," I said, my voice shaking, "will this darkness, this rain, this storm freeze us to death? Is this how we are destined to die?"

He shut his book and put it in his bag. He took out the stub of a candle and lit it. A dim light illuminated the room, casting our shadows on the walls. As the flame flickered in the wind, our shadows trembled.

Swami Ji gently caressed my face and said, "What are you scared of? All this is an illusion."

"An illusion?" I didn't understand what he meant.

"This night, this darkness, this cold – all this is nothing but a dream."

"But it looks real to me." I was truly surprised.

"That doesn't matter," Swami Ji laughed. "Doesn't everything look real in a dream?"

I nodded in agreement.

"Likewise, this room, these windows without panes, this rain, this biting cold – all this is a dream . . . maya. When you wake up tomorrow, none of this will be here – not these mountains, not this journey, not our fellow passengers."

He got up, put his shoes on, opened the door and went outside – perhaps to relieve himself. I, too, stood up and returned to my spot. Swami Ji's words had consoled me greatly, and slowly the fear in my heart began to subside. Actually, fear is not around us. It is inside us. We just need to calm our minds.

As I was thinking about all this, Makhan drew his head out from under the blanket and asked, "What was he saying to you? That all this is a dream?" I nodded. "You should have asked him who is having this dream. Him? You? Or are all of us are dreaming the same dream together?"

He retreated into his blanket and went back to sleep. I was alone again. Just then, a gust of wind snuffed out the candle, and once more, that old fear crept into my heart. The terrifying scene of the mountain collapsing flashed before my eyes. I wrapped myself in the blanket and lay down, but I was too disturbed to sleep. I got up and lit a cigarette.

I wish it were a dream, I began to think . . . But what does 'were a dream' mean? It *is* a dream. Swami Ji wasn't wrong. If it wasn't a dream or an illusion, what was it? Take Swami Ji or Makhan . . . I hadn't known them before today. But at this moment, my world shrunk to only these two. When I got home tomorrow, or as Swami Ji said, when I awoke from the dream, they would no longer be there.

The lit end of the cigarette touched my left arm and I felt a burning sensation . . . But how does it matter? One can feel anything. What is wet can feel dry and what is dry can feel wet. It's not necessary that what we feel is real.

I shook Makhan. He woke up. I asked him, "Makhan can you tell what reality is?"

"The reality is that we are all cowards." He seemed ready with an answer to my question.

"Do you know why the driver stopped here for the night? He gets paid extra. It doesn't matter if we freeze to death, he will get his money. All he cares about is money. He doesn't give a damn about anything else. It's a shame that we could do nothing about it."

"But what if all this really turns out to be a dream? What will you say then?"

"I'll say: So what? If we had all pressed the driver to continue with the journey, we would be home by now, resting in our own warm beds. This dream would not be so disturbing."

Makhan seemed ready with an answer again.

I was even more confused. He could be right about us being cowards. It was also possible that Swami Ji was right about it all being a dream. When we wake up tomorrow, these mountains will not exist, nor the rain, nor the wind, nor the biting cold . . . But it is a long time until morning. For now, it is night. For now, it is dark. For now, it is cold. In this darkness and this cold, I am alone. Of the two people here, the one who has covered himself with the blanket is upset with me, and the other, who does not feel the cold, is still outside.

The Mourners

TARZAN'S SISTER-IN-LAW WAS TRYING TO LIGHT THE OVEN. SHE had been huffing and puffing in vain to get the fire started, but the sodden logs and cow dung pats refused to burn. The ground floor was filled with smoke.

"Where is he?" Doctor asked her.

Seeing him filled her with such rage that she felt like taking a smouldering log from the half-lit fire and thrashing both Doctor and Tarzan. Why has he come on this cold winter morning to lure my brother-in-law out, she thought. It's not his fault entirely, my own brother law is in cahoots with him.

"Is he still asleep?" asked Doctor. He assumed from her silence that he was right and continued up the stairs. He heard her pacing about but paid no attention.

"Get up, you lazy bum. Pedro is free at last," he shouted as he entered the room.

Tarzan woke up with a start. He hadn't quite understood what Doctor had said, but he guessed that something had happened.

"His mother died," said Doctor as he sat down beside him.

Tarzan reached out from under his quilt to open the window, and the room slowly filled with the faint morning light. The quilt was covered with a ragged blanket over which Tarzan had spread his phĕrăn. His pillow, printed with red flowers, was coverless and had been soaking up his hair oil for years. To his right were colorful pictures of film actresses cut out from magazines, and to his left lay a packet containing two and a half cigarettes.

"When?"

"This morning, apparently," said Doctor as he took a cigarette from Tarzan's packet and lit it with his kāngĕr. "She must have passed away at some time during the night, but that asshole only noticed in the morning because he was out having a good time."

"That rascal! Without us?"

"I didn't know either. I heard that they were all having fun at Patwari's house. There were some strangers there too."

"What? He'll be ruined! How did he end up there? They gamble night and day in that place. Give me a cigarette." Doctor took another cigarette from Tarzan's pack and gave it to him.

"Pass me the kāngĕr."

Doctor handed it over. Tarzan lit the cigarette and put the kāngĕr under his quilt. "He's alone, now. His mother used to always get in the way. So now that her ship has sailed, he can sell his house and gamble everything away."

"I bet he'll do exactly that."

"Okay, so what do we do now?"

"We'll have to carry Pedro's mother's body to the cremation ground. Come on, gird your loins!"

"Girded! Tell me, who else's mothers and fathers need to be borne forth?"

Tarzan got up and put on his phĕrăn. He picked up a comb from the shelf, slicked his hair back, wrapped his head in a muffler, extracted three pairs of socks from under his pillow and pulled them on. Then he handed his kāngĕr to Doctor and said, "Right, let's go."

"Wait, let's finish the cigarette first." Doctor stoked the kāngĕr with his bare hands and wiped them on the inside of his phĕrăn.

"Sure. The old woman was never in any hurry, no need to rush now."

Tarzan picked his kāngĕr from the shelf where he had left it the previous night and shook it. Lumps of coal rose to the surface. He took a burning ember from Doctor's kāngĕr and blew on it to light his own.

"Aren't you going to get fresh charcoal?" Doctor asked him.

"I'll fill it up with a shovelful of embers at the baker's shop. I don't want to ask for a favour so early in the morning. Hey, what's the score?"

"Who the fuck knows."

"If they can take six wickets today, they might win."

"As if they're going to win," said Doctor, making an obscene gesture. "It's not like they've won anywhere else."

They left the room. Doctor went back for the half cigarette left in the pack and stuck it behind his ear.

"Why leave this behind?" he said.

They went downstairs and came out through the corridor without a sound.

Tarzan's sister-in-law was standing in the doorway. As they stepped on to the porch, she shouted at them again, "Does he care? When dawn breaks, he leaves home dressed like a gentleman, with his hair oiled, eats every meal without caring where it comes from. I am the one who has to bear the burden . . . alone!"

"Where, oh where did your brother find this exotic bird?" Doctor asked Tarzan as they headed down the street.

"Come on, at least he was lucky enough to find one – we can't hope for even that much."

"You might not find anyone. I, on the other hand, am in love."

Tarzan examined him from head to foot and said, "Not a chance."

He filled his kāngĕr with freshly lit mulberry coal from the baker's shop in the market. He took three packs of cigarettes on credit from a grocery shop and told Doctor, "Now I can carry the entire city to the cremation ground on my shoulders. I'm all set."

"Did you ask the baker the score?"

"His transistor has run out of batteries." He took two cigarettes from a pack, lit one for himself and gave the other to Doctor. Doctor threw away the half cigarette he had tucked behind his ear.

"I wanted to listen to the cricket commentary today. Who knew that this misfortune was waiting for us? What time do you think we'll be done?"

"One or two o'clock."

"Should we listen to the commentary or . . . ?" Tarzan remembered something. "Hey, what film is showing uptown?" he asked.

"Some rubbish."

"What about downtown?"

"Boring."

"Okay, and what about in that other place?"

"Can't say. It opened only yesterday."

"What about across town?"

"I heard it's good."

"Let's go if we get done by one. Otherwise, we'll listen to the cricket commentary."

"Do you think they'll win?"

"If they win, I'll buy you a meal – I swear on your life."

Pedro had shed no tears when he found his mother dead. He had gone straight to Pahalwan. Pahalwan took the news first to Setha and then to the priest. On the way, he saw Doctor's brother and sent word to Doctor. Setha took fifty rupees and went to buy a shroud and other things needed for a funeral. Pedro began to wail only after Setha returned with the funeral material and a few neighbors had gathered.

Pedro had no immediate family in the city, except for the husband of a maternal cousin who lived five or six miles away. Pedro did not inform him of the death. Even if Pedro had told him, he wouldn't have come. Pedro loathed all his relations, both in the city and in the villages. The truth was that it was his mother who had kept up with the family. Now that she had died, those ties were finally severed. He was free not just in this one way, but in all senses. He had no obligation to greet his relatives, to perform the memorial ritual for his deceased father each year, or even to come home every night. He was free to do whatever he wanted. From this point on, he was master of his own destiny and owner of his house.

After about an hour, Pahalwan arrived with the priest. A woman from the neighborhood filled a vessel with water for bathing the corpse and put it on the fire. After a part of the courtyard was prepared for the funeral ceremonies, the priest began to perform the last rites with Pedro. Pedro was still in the process of moving the sacred thread from one shoulder to another when Tarzan and Doctor arrived.

Tarzan went straight to Pedro and whispered, "Have you got any money?"

"Yes, I do."

"Do you swear on your mother's life?"

"Yes, I've got money. May my mother die if I lie."

"All right, then." Tarzan sat on a stone mortar on one side of the courtyard. When it was time to wash the corpse, he got up and said to Pahalwan, "This old woman turned out to be very selfish. She is bathing with warm water while poor Pedro will have to wash himself in the freezing water of the river in this cold winter."

After the body had been bathed, it was wrapped in a shroud and placed on a bier. Tarzan and Setha lifted the front of the bier on to their shoulders. Doctor took the third corner and Pahalwan was about to take the fourth when Doctor stopped him. "Hey, mleccha! Don't touch the bier, the corpse will get polluted."

"She'll jump off the bier if she finds out that a Muslim is carrying her corpse," said Tarzan.

"Well, give her a ride yourself then!" Pahalwan stepped back. "But remember, the keeper of the pyre is always a Muslim."

"What do you care?" retorted Setha.

In the end, a young boy from the neighborhood took the fourth corner of the bier, and the procession set off for the cremation ground.

Pedro walked in front with the funerary basket in his hands. The priest who was alongside Pedro had covered himself from head to toe in a blanket. He was annoyed at having to leave his house so early in the cold morning. He thought to himself, A lawyer can say no, a doctor can say no, but we can never say no. This profession be damned. I'm not even sure if this wretch can pay my fee.

Tarzan, Setha, Doctor, and the young boy from the neighborhood followed Pedro and the priest with the dead body. Pahalwan brought up the rear along with some neighbors who turned back after a few hundred yards.

Pedro walked straight ahead with the basket. That morning, he had felt free. His mother had died. But now, he realized that he was not free at all. He had simply been let loose. The knot that had bound him to the shore had been cut. He could either float aim-lessly in the world or drown. He could be marooned in the shallows and rot there, or he could remain adrift for as long as he was alive. Mother used to curse him, but she also prayed for him. She would pester him by demanding money for household expenses, but at the end of each month she would give him money for cigarettes. Often, she would be annoyed with him, yet at times she hugged him tight. From now on, he would neither get on anyone's nerves, nor would he be missed by anyone. He would mourn for no one, and his death would not be mourned either. He was alone in the world now, and the world was cruel.

Suddenly, he looked back and felt as if the ground beneath his feet had slipped away. He was walking alone with the basket in his hand. There was no sign of the priest or the bier with his dead mother or of all those who were carrying it. What calamity is this, he wondered. In his panic, the basket almost fell from his hand, but he grasped it tightly to his chest. Was he dreaming? Or was God testing him with an illusion?

When he found the priest lighting a cigarette at a shop, he felt he could breathe again. But where had the rest of them gone? Where was his mother? Had the earth gobbled them up? Had the sky swallowed them all? The priest came up with a lit cigarette and said to Pedro, "Something inauspicious is about to happen. They could have slipped on the way and the dead body may have fallen. It's a bad omen."

Pedro had a premonition of something evil. The priest's words added nothing to that, but the question remained – where were the rest of them? Even if they had slipped, they couldn't have flown away and disappeared. Something peculiar must have happened. The priest recited loudly, "Forgive me my sins, O Shiva Shambhu, O Mahadev Shambhu!" The lamp burning in the basket had gone out some time ago, and a line of smoke plumed from the half-burnt wick. Pedro was confused and anxious. His terrified heart was racing.

At last, he saw the hazy outline of the bier carrying his mother's dead body approaching.

"Three have fallen," Tarzan shouted as he came nearer.

"You mean that the dead body fell three times? God save us!" the priest cried out in fright.

"No! My favorite bowler has taken three wickets."

"Shut up!" Setha bit back his anger.

"I swear by the Prophet, this is terrible," Pahalwan said to Pedro.

"Look, Tarzan stopped at Shorty's, the paan seller's, and said that he wanted to listen to the cricket commentary. We told him to keep walking. The paan seller too begged him to keep going. But Tarzan just stayed where he was. We stood there with the dead body for at least ten minutes. Even the traffic stopped," said Pahalwan.

"For the past seventy years, she was never in any hurry. How do these ten minutes matter?" Tarzan said.

"Someone shut him up." Setha was trembling with rage. "If he doesn't shut his mouth, I will leave the dead body and be on my way."

The priest lashed out at Pedro. "Are you human beings or animals? I swear that from now on I will never . . . Oh, but you don't have anyone else . . ."

When they reached the cremation ground on the banks of the river, Tarzan, Setha, Doctor, and the young boy from Pedro's neighborhood lowered the weight from their shoulders. The cremator started piling up the wood to make a pyre. Pedro began to recite the funeral prayers along with the priest.

Tarzan stretched his arms and announced, "Hey, did you hear? Doctor's in love."

Pahalwan and Setha burst out laughing.

"With whom?" Pahalwan asked.

"I'll tell you," Tarzan replied. "He's in love with his boss."

The young boy from the neighborhood blushed.

"He does all her housework – irons her clothes, folds her saris, buys her groceries from the market. Do you get anything in return, or are you just wasting your energy on her chores?"

Doctor snapped, "I'll break your teeth if you go on with this nonsense. She's like a mother to me."

"Why are you teasing him? You visit the owner of the printing press at his house," Pahalwan said to Tarzan.

"Crap! You think I'm angling for a promotion, just because I visit his house? I have some self-respect. I'm not like you, writing a letter of apology!"

"Did Pahalwan write an apology? Has he stopped throwing his weight around?" Doctor asked.

"What else could he do?" Tarzan said. "The police arrested him for something involving an illegal poster. But his neighbors and relatives spread the rumour that he'd been arrested for theft."

"What else could I do if not write that letter of apology?" said Pahalwan.

"Don't say letter of apology, say you signed a bond," Doctor corrected him.

Setha started laughing.

"So, Lord Tansen, when are you going to sing at the radio station?" Tarzan turned to Setha.

"Enough! Don't mock me. I won't stand for it." Setha was truly upset. Tarzan, Pahalwan, and Doctor started laughing.

The pyre had almost gone out. The flames were low, and the crackling of the glowing embers grew louder. Pedro sat with his head down, lost in thought.

"Get up, let's go." Setha put his hand on Pedro's shoulder. "Come on, get up."

Pedro got up.

"It was warm and cosy here. Well, we'll come too," Doctor said.

"This is a disaster. Winter has almost ended and there's no sign of snow," Pahalwan said.

"If there had been a snowfall, it wouldn't be this cold."

"Where's Tarzan?" Pedro asked.

Everyone looked around, but he was nowhere to be seen.

"He must have left already," Setha said.

"Useless chap. Wanted to listen to the cricket commentary. As if his brothers-in-law were playing."

"He's never touched a cricket bat and has no idea of mid-on and silly mid-on. And still he's gone off without his friends." Pahalwan was also angry.

"Maybe he didn't go to listen to the commentary, maybe he went to watch a movie," Doctor said. "He's been restless all morning."

Pedro, Doctor, and Setha bowed before the pyre and were about to leave, when Pahalwan exclaimed, "That asshole's still here!"

Tarzan was standing behind a chinar tree, gazing at the pyre.

"We thought you'd slipped away," Doctor said. Tarzan said nothing.

"Aren't you coming?" Pahalwan asked him. Tarzan still did not respond.

"Come on, now. There's nothing to stay for," Pedro said.

Tarzan's eyes filled with tears and he embraced Pedro. "Six years ago, I carried my own mother here and burned her to ashes."

Both of them began to wail loudly, like women.

Witnessing this, Doctor and Pahalwan were stunned. But Setha counseled them to not say anything. "This is the despair death invites. Let them cry."

A Song of Despair

THE SCORCHING SUMMER SUN IS BEARABLE BUT HOW CAN ONE possibly withstand this oppressive humidity? It makes you want to strip naked and wander in the streets.

Not a whisper of a breeze. It was as if someone was holding the wind captive. I felt restless. I got up and sat on the window ledge with my legs dangling outside. It was eleven at night, but sleep, upset with me, was hiding far away.

Across the alley, in Roop Ji's room, a musical performance was in full swing and the place was alive with the sound of the sitar, the tabla, the sarangi, and other instruments. Occasionally, when the music stopped, the room echoed with applause or with Roop Ji's raucous laughter. Soon, the music would take over again.

Roop Ji laughed exactly like his father. When Kishan Chand

laughed, children in the neighborhood would awaken from their sleep. But now that he had grown old, his laughter sounded hollow. My aunt used to say, ten or fifteen years ago, his laughter would startle new brides and rattle the windows of our house. That devil, even his laughter reverberated like the high-pitched drumming of a tabla.

In the room, Roop Ji was singing accompanied by his friends Gir Chakri and Rajnath on the tabla and the sarangi. I heard two unfamiliar voices as well and, from the conversation in the room, I gathered that they belonged to a certain Khan Sahib and a Pandit Ji. I could not see Kishan Chand in the room. Were he here I would still be able to hear his singing or laughter. Perhaps he is unwell; people are bothered by minor ailments in old age.

Kishan Chand loved to sing. Not only was he an enthusiastic singer, he was also one of a small group of people who founded a Kashmiri theater troupe forty years ago. In those days actors were not respected or considered the artists or performers that they are today. They were scoffed at and called names. But what could be more worthwhile than to fulfill one's heart's desire? Braving all criticism, the group had successfully staged plays such as *Satyawaan* and *Satyawadi Harish Chandra* one after the other.

My uncle says that, in his youth, he had also wanted to act in these plays. He had expressed this desire to Kishan Chand who had interviewed him at the group's office.

"Have you ever pulled the turban off your father's head on an auspicious day?" This was the very first question Kishan Chand had asked my uncle.

"I asked if you have ever, on any auspicious occasion, such as Shivaratri, New Year's or on his birthday, pulled off your father's turban?"

My uncle shook his head vigorously.

"Okay, if not on a special day, have you ever done this noble deed on any ordinary day?"

"What noble deed?"

"Pulled off your father Raghu Joo's turban?"

"Who does that?" my uncle retorted.

"Sometimes one has to do it. If you haven't already done so, do you think that you could do it any time in the future?"

"No, I can't do something so disrespectful," my uncle replied, suppressing his anger.

"Then you cannot act. We regret that your application is rejected."

My uncle says the next day, Kishan Chand came to his home and consoled him, "Did I offend you? I didn't intend to. Look, next month we are rehearsing a new play, *Anarkali*. You are a good-looking guy with striking features. We could offer you the role of Prince Saleem and I will be Akbar the Great and say, 'Sheikhu! This is not the emperor Akbar commanding you but a helpless father pleading before his son.' Your response would be, 'Emperor Akbar! Love is a like a great flood. It will destroy even a father if he comes in its way.'

"Let us suppose that, you are delivering this line, and your eyes fall upon your father Raghu Joo sitting in the audience. Tell me sincerely, would you be able to say this? The moment you see Raghu Joo you will lose your wits. How could you possibly say lines that talk about destroying your father? You must lose your inhibitions before you can act, and pull that turban off his head!"

My uncle couldn't pull off his father's turban and so did not become an actor. Instead, he volunteered in the forestry department for six months until he was appointed a clerk there for a monthly salary of twelve rupees. He got married, had children – a son and two daughters – got all three of them married, performed the sacred thread ceremonies for his grandsons and other religious ceremonies for his granddaughters. In short, he did all that is expected of every respectable and well-bred Brahmin.

But Kishan Chand had indeed brought dishonor to his father. Sri Kak Tikoo, his father, was a land revenue officer. He was well-known and dreaded throughout the city. Kishan Chand was born after two marriages and four daughters. His father's wish had been that Kishan Chand should become a revenue advisor, or a minister in the government. However, Kishan Chand was unable to pass the entrance exam. When he failed for the third time, Sri Kak stopped talking to him. The son endured his father's sulking for two days. On the third day he set up shop selling tobacco and paper fans on the street right opposite their home, much to the horror of the whole neighborhood. Such a worthless son born to such a noble father! In those days, if anyone mocked Kishan Chand, asking him, "Kish Kak, what has happened to you?" he would respond humbly, "Oh nothing, it's just that Sri Kak, the revenue inspector, has gone bankrupt." In the end, Sri Kak asked his brothers-in-law and son-in-law to mediate. Seven days later, Kishan Chand was made to shut the shop and brought home.

Roop Ji stopped singing and was now plucking the strings of the sitar. Gir accompanied him on the tabla and Rajnath played the sarangi intermittently. Pandit Ji and Khan Sahib were engrossed and expressed their pleasure by swaying their heads from side to side. Though not local, I presumed that they were both accomplished musicians and that Roop Ji had invited them over so that he could display his own talent. Khan Sahib seemed impressed by Roop Ji. He exclaimed "Subhanallah" from time to time and exchanged meaningful glances with Pandit Ji, perhaps trying to say, "I had no idea this young man was so accomplished and capable of evoking such emotion in his music."

I watched all of this while sitting on my windowsill. Only a narrow lane separated Roop Ji's room from mine. I had switched off my lights but the tube light in his room created an illusion of broad daylight. Because of the heat, all three windows were open and the curtains were drawn wide. It was as if I were sitting in a dark corner of a concert hall watching a musical performance on a brightly illuminated stage. Roop Ji's playing sent me into raptures, though I did not understand all the nuances of these various compositions. The suffocation from the terrible heat and humidity that felt like a rope strangling me started to loosen and an unfamiliar calm began to settle upon my heart. It was as though the Aharbal waterfall was cascading in front of me. The sound of the gushing waters echoed in my ears while the ice-cold droplets splashed my burning cheeks. My eyes attempted to arrest the flowing waters, but the waterfall tore itself free. Eventually, the water seemed to still and I started to rise, higher and higher, extremely high, till I began to feel drowsy.

At that very moment, the music stopped and the room reverberated with applause. I saw Khan Sahib embrace Roop Ji and kiss his forehead. Roop Ji got up, opened the cupboard, and took out a bottle of liquor and filled plates with walnuts, almonds, and fried snacks. Rajnath fetched glasses from the table and Gir Chakri took out some apples and began to peel them.

Suddenly, my eyes were drawn to the porch, where I saw Kishan Chand. He was sitting with his head in his hands and seemed very disappointed. A musical celebration upstairs in Roop Ji's room, and Kishan Chand sitting downstairs in the porch in despair! This was something new. The impossible had happened. It seemed he was not happy with the performances. Yet he had devoted his entire life to this music. Perhaps he understood that such soirées would lead to carousing and other illicit activities. But he himself was no teetotaller. It was rumored that he had taken to drinking early in his youth.

My aunt claims, "One day, at about six or seven o'clock, Kishan Chand visited us. He came to chat with your uncle. I had been married for only two or three years. Back then, Kishan Chand with his green eyes looked like an Englishman. But that day his eyes sparkled more than ever and he looked exceedingly handsome. Once he was done talking, he began to sing. Your uncle was bored, but the song pierced my heart. I put out the stove and immersed myself in the song with my chin in my hand. It was as if the goddess Saraswati herself lived in his throat and the song sounded like the tinkling of bells. I realized that I had not offered him tea. As if he had come to a Muslim household! I got up to prepare tea in the samovar. I went upstairs and took some cardamom and almonds from the spice chest, added them to the tea, and offered the cup to him. But he refused it. Covering my face with the sleeve of my phĕrăn, I insisted, but to no avail. Instead he got up quickly, put on his shoes and left. When he was gone, your uncle said, 'How could he have had tea? The scoundrel! He was drunk!' I had no idea how your uncle assumed this. I didn't think so. Can a drunk sound so melodious? He is more likely to lose himself or become abusive. I don't think he was drunk. And even if he were, how does that matter? I swear upon my son Nath and you that I kept that cup of tea for three whole days. I couldn't bring myself to serve it to anyone else."

I too had seen Kishan Chand drink on many occasions. But what is wrong with drinking? If I could afford to, I would also drink. But I don't have a job. I am not only without work, but I am an orphan as well. It is only because of my uncle's and my aunt's generosity that I get two meals a day. A person can drink only if he has the money.

Kishan Chand had money. Roop Ji also was wealthy. Kishan Chand never had a job but Roop Ji is a lecturer and his wife a schoolteacher. He has his inheritance from his grandfather too. Is it a crime if he drank? Kishan Chand shouldn't be so upset with his son. Could there be more to this than meets the eye?

Let it be, I thought to myself, why do I care? Why should I get involved in the affairs of others? But no. I can't sleep, therefore, I need to keep my mind busy. I must keep thinking about something – anything. All day long I keep thinking of my own problems. So what if I poke around in other people's affairs now? Anything to pass the night.

Kishan Chand's wife, Arandhati also came out on the porch and sat next to him. They both seemed gloomy. Kishan Chand had married Arandhati when he was thirty years old and she barely fifteen. Kishan Chand had stayed single until he was thirty even though it was customary for Hindu boys to be married by the age of twelve or thirteen. Was Kishan Chand reluctant to marry, or had his father deliberately delayed his marriage? Or had it simply not been possible to find a suitable match because he lived such an unsettled life?

Once, while away on a trip to Vothros village, he returned after seven days with a bride. Some people said that Arandhati was a widow; others said that she was neither widowed nor abandoned; rather, she belonged to a low-caste family. Kishan Chand had seen her bathing in a stream and had offered five hundred rupees for her hand in marriage. Very few people knew the truth, but Sri Kak was humiliated. He summoned his extended family and decided to publicly disown his son. But Kishan Chand had already left home and rented a room at the house of a neighboring widow. He returned two days before Sri Kak's death, but only after his whole family pleaded with him to forget all past differences and to offer his dying father the last sip of holy water.

"What a lucky woman Arandhati was!" my aunt often remarked.

"Had Kishan Chand not married her in secret, she would be scavenging for food with stray dogs. She would have been in a desperate condition. Look how he loves her, as if she is a queen. It is also true that sometimes he hits her, beats her brutally. But I have seen with my own eyes, Kishan Chand sits her in his lap and feeds her pieces of rogan josh. And look at your uncle, he neither quarrels nor expresses any affection for me. He is completely indifferent."

Roop Ji stood up and poured another round of drinks. After two or three sips, Khan Sahib rose and poured some of his own drink into Roop Ji's glass. He held the glass up to his eyes in reverence and then gulped the drink down. Khan Sahib embraced him, and Roop Ji wept and tears rolled down his cheeks.

Kishan Chand and his wife sat quietly on the porch downstairs. "How long can he sit there sulking?" I thought to myself. For some reason, I assumed that he would get up and go into Roop Ji's room like a lion barging into a flock of sheep. That he would kick Roop Ji, saying, "Do you know how to drink? Go suck on your mother's breast" and then say to Khan Sahib, "Khan Sahib hamare saath piyo." He would then take the bottle out from his phĕrăn pocket, pour half of it into a glass for Khan Sahib and gulp the rest down. He would shove Rajnath away, snatch the tabla from him, and play it so vigorously that the entire street would shake with its dha-dha-tir-kit-tir-kit-gha-na. Then his hands would pick up speed so that the whole neighborhood would begin dancing nigan-nigan-tikat-ghing.

Knowing Kishan Chand's temperament, this is what should have happened. However, it didn't. Kishan Chand was still brooding, with his head in his hands. Arandhati wanted to say something, but she dared not speak. Finally, she gathered her courage and said, "Get up now, go to sleep. How long will you sit here like this?"

"You whore! Why don't you shut up?" Kishan Chand replied angrily. "Go inside if you feel sleepy, go to bed. How does it matter if you lie alone tonight? Poor Sheela Ji is sitting in the kitchen, weeping over her fate. And how can I possibly sleep?"

"You misunderstood me. I can't possibly face her. My heart breaks to see her in this state," Arandhati cried, wiping her eyes with her scarf.

"Have Bittu Ji and Lovely slept?" Kishan Chand asked.

"I put them both to bed. Poor Lovely went to sleep without eating."

"What else could she do? After all, it is her misfortune to be born in my house."

I lay on the bed, but still felt restless. How long would this oppressive heat last? When would it rain? How happy we feel when summer arrives and frees us from the trials of winter. But then that same summer becomes unbearable. Its delights and pleasures soon disappear, and it weighs heavily on our hearts. We get frustrated. I got up and drank a full glass of water, but that too felt like it was boiling. Finally, I switched off the lights and jumped into bed.

Roop Ji had been passionate about singing since his childhood. Singing was in his blood, in the very essence of his being. When he completed his bachelor's in science, his father sent him to Roorkee to study engineering. He failed the first semester twice. Later, it was discovered that he had skipped out of both college and hostel, and spent most of his time nineteen miles away playing tambourine and cymbals with the sadhus in Haridwar. Then Kishan Chand sent him to study for a master's in chemistry. Roop Ji managed to last there for two years and passed his final examination with a second division. Only during the practical exam did he do something strange. But with God's grace even that served him well. It was rumoured that, while he was busy in the laboratory, someone outside had switched on a radio and a great maestro was singing a *thumri*. Roop Ji forgot that he was in the middle of a practical exam for his master's degree. He drifted along with the song. When the examiner came to check his progress, Roop Ji suggested, with a finger on his lips, that he keep quiet. This offended the examiner and he would have done something terrible – then, at that moment the singer sang *"Ab ke sawan ghar aa"* and emphasized at *"aa"* in such a way that Roop Ji was unable to control himself. He swayed his head and started to drum on the table with his palm such that the test tube filled with acid tipped over, burning his hand. There was an uproar in the laboratory. The examiner was sympathetic to Roop Ji's predicament and graded him generously.

Roop Ji didn't bother looking for a job when he finished his degree. Instead, he rented a room from the Auqaaf Trust in the market and started Roop Sangeet Sadan, a school for music. Kishan Chand was not pleased. He tried to reason with his son. "See, it was different with me. I was illiterate and a vagabond but you have a MSc. I'm not asking you to give up music. Music is a great art – the worship of goddess Saraswati herself. But singing in the street is a little embarrassing. You have to marry and bring someone's daughter to this house. And it's not only about you. Usha too has to be married off."

Roop Ji did not agree with his father. He continued to hang out all day long with Rajnath, Gir Chakri, Brij Wugra and Khursheed Peer at Roop Sangeet Sadan and at four o'clock he would go to Ameera Kadal to give music lessons to a Sikh girl. Meanwhile, Kishan Chand kept trying to find him a job, meeting officers and ministers from time to time. One day Arandhati visited our house with a plate full of puris, to announce that Roop Ji had been appointed a professor in Amar Singh College. That same evening, my aunt fought with my uncle and taunted him. "You used to say that Kishan Chand has ruined his children. But look he managed to get his son a job as a professor. And you can't even manage a small promotion for our son Nath. Anyway, who knows you? Kishan Chand is famous; the whole world knows him. The other day a photograph of him playing the sitar even appeared in the newspaper. Here you are, no one knows your name beyond the cosmetic shop in this alley."

I got up, sat on the window ledge again and looked towards Kishan Chand's house. There was no one on the porch. Both husband and wife had gone inside. Upstairs Pandit Ji was singing with Roop Ji accompanying him on the tabla. I have no idea what he was singing. Occasionally I caught the line *"Lage naahi nayan,"* I can't sleep a wink. These were the only three words that my ears and my mind registered. I am bored but what can I do? I am restless. It's midnight and I can't fall asleep. I can't close my eyes. *Lage naahi nayan.*

Suddenly, I heard Arandhati scream and then Kishan Chand shout, 'Sheela Ji! Sheela Ji! Have a sip of water.' I gathered that Roop Ji's wife had fainted again. Everyone in the neighborhood knew that Roop Ji was unwilling to marry her, but his parents, and especially his sister and brother-in-law had forced him. Roop Ji's prospective father-in-law, who was a deputy secretary, had got him the job. People say that, first the date for the marriage was fixed and then the appointment letter for the job was finalized. Kishan Chand threw a lavish wedding party for his son. A feast was arranged for a full week. When the bride arrived, the entire house was decorated with lights. My aunt also went to see the bride, but she was not impressed. When she returned, she told me that Kishan Chand had not found a suitable bride for his son. "He deserved better. She looks worn out and is probably older than him. If Arandhati were made-up like a bride she would look younger than this daughter-in-law. In short, Kishan Chand seems to have been swayed by the family's wealth."

Kishan Chand once again came out on to the porch with his hookah. He started smoking and it sounded like he was playing the jal tarang with other musical instruments in Roop Ji's room. I felt that he was in a trance and when Arandhati came out it looked as if he had just been jolted from a dream.

"Has she recovered?" he asked Arandhati.

"Yes, she has. I asked her to lie down in our room – but she refuses," Arandhati replied.

"Someday, she is going to collapse," he sighed.

Arandhati sighed as well.

"I think I am responsible for all her suffering. She didn't deserve this wretch of a man. Actually, it's my fault. I should have let him marry that Sikh girl."

"There is no way I would have let that happen. Why piss in a pitcher of milk and bring shame to our family!" Arandhati replied.

Sounds of loud cheers came from the room upstairs. Pandit Ji had finished singing and now Khan Sahib picked up the sitar. It was as if his fingers were not only plucking the strings but also dancing to the rhythm. Pandit Ji accompanied him on the tabla. For some reason, Khan Sahib's singing caused me more anguish . . . I felt as if I would scream. I was agitated and came inside and threw myself on the bed. The night had begun to fade, but my restlessness had not. Usually if I couldn't sleep through the night, I would at least close my eyes at dawn. But tonight sleep was certainly upset with me, hiding far away. The heat, and humidity too, hadn't ebbed. Summers are like this: the days burn you and the nights boil you; evenings suffocate you and the mornings bring no relief.

The Tongue and the Egg

T
HE DOOR WAS LOCKED FROM THE INSIDE. I PEERED THROUGH the window slats and was startled. The room was dark, but a small ray of light from the porthole fell on the spot where my friend was tied to a post. A piece of cloth was stuffed into his mouth. His clothes were torn to shreds. As my eyes grew accustomed to the darkness, I observed other things. Two young men were searching the room. They were examining the floor, emptying the baskets, and breaking open the trunks. One of the men was short and the other tall. But both were dressed alike in khaki trousers, cream-colored shirts, and cherry-red sweaters. Despite turning the room over, it did not look like they had found what they were searching for.

They untied my friend and bent down to retie the laces of their shoes tightly. I realized that they were getting ready to leave. I shifted slightly to the right and stood against the wall. They opened the door and came out. Once outside, they looked around carefully. As soon as they saw me their eyes flashed with anger. Using my wits, I pulled a pack of cigarettes from my pocket and offered them one. The short one smirked and, taking out a matchbox, lit my cigarette, then that of his companion and his own. I went inside and they sat down on the door ledge.

I hugged my friend tightly and asked him what had happened. But how could he have answered. The cloth was still stuffed into his mouth. I turned and looked beseechingly at the two young men. The short one got up and pulled the cloth from my friend's mouth. He folded the handkerchief carefully and placed it in his pocket. I kissed his hand in gratitude and then moved back to my friend and whispered

"What is this all about?"

He did not reply. Suspicious, I forced his mouth open with my two hands and indeed his tongue was missing. Assuming a friendly manner, I put my hand in the short man's pocket and asked,

"What is the point of playing with this man? Let him be and give it back to him."

"Give what back to him?" he asked flicking the cigarette from his fingers.

"His tongue, of course," I said as I passed him another cigarette.

"But I swear I have not taken his tongue. Here look at this hand-kerchief," and he took the folded piece of cloth out of his pocket and showed it to me. I grasped the handkerchief and shook it. I was convinced that my friend's tongue would fall out. But there was nothing in the handkerchief. I then searched the man's pockets but they too were empty.

"Maybe he's hidden it himself and is trying to blame us," said the short one as he lit his cigarette.

"Where would he hide it? Wouldn't it rot? If he owned a fridge, it would be a different story. Many wealthy people have stored their tongues in their fridges for safekeeping. They will be preserved and taken out when needed. If you have taken it please give it back to this poor man." I pleaded with him, and searched his pockets again.

Meanwhile the tall man approached us. Seeing me with my hands in his friend's pockets made him angry. He scolded me, "What the hell would we want with his tongue. We were looking for eggs."

"Eggs?" I asked in amazement.

"Yes, we have to collect six million eggs. We have only managed to get three million so far."

"But what for?"

"What do you mean what for?" the men said and burst out laughing.

"I swear I have no idea what you are talking about," I said seriously.

The short man took pity on me and my ignorance and said, "The new mansion will need marble chips; the mortar mixture will have to be prepared with egg whites. This will ensure floors that shine better."

"Whose new mansion?" I asked again. My question seemed to amuse them even more and they doubled up in laughter, holding on to each other.

"Whose mansion he asks?" they said and laughed again.

Dejected, I came back to my friend who was mending his torn clothes.

"Do you know whose new house this is?" I asked quietly. He did not reply.

"All right, were you informed that your house would be searched for eggs?" He did not reply. Belatedly, I remembered that he could not speak. I felt stupid and started to slink away with my head down. The short man grabbed my arm and asked if I was leaving.

"What else can I do?" I said.

"Are you just going to stand by and watch this atrocity?"

"What do you mean 'atrocity'?"

"Look," the tall man explained, "had we found eggs here we would have taken them. What would he have eaten and how would he have fed his children?"

"Well, you didn't find eggs and he doesn't have children," I interrupted.

"Had he had children, we would definitely have found eggs here and we would have seized them. His children would have starved and died young. Is that not cruel?"

"But what can I do?" I asked.

"You have to speak out against this injustice," said the tall man as he stood up. He appeared to have grown even taller. I wondered how he had entered the house through the small doorway. The short man raised himself on his toes and asked, "Why don't you raise your voice?"

I summoned every bit of courage in my body and asked, "Why don't you protest about this?"

"What can we do? Our job is to raid people's homes and collect six million eggs. Our hands are tied," replied the short man. The tall one started wailing.

"When we go to search an innocent person's house, when we take eggs from hen coops, when we rummage through people's clothes, in case they have hidden the eggs, we ourselves are shaken."

I kissed his forehead and wiped his tears with the handkerchief I took out of my pocket.

"Please wipe my nose too," he sobbed.

I wiped his nose and then asked, "What should we do now?" He turned around and asked his companion the same question.

"I don't know what to say," was the response. "There is a holy man here, why don't we ask him?"

We entered a small stone house. Inside, on a carpeted floor was a straw hut. The holy man, wearing red pajamas and a green shirt, was resting propped up on pillows. His white, flowing beard reached down to his feet. In front of him were piles of almonds and cardamom pods. A disciple wearing a black sherwani and a grey turban was massaging his feet. I touched the holy man's feet and then looked up at him and begged, "My Lord, horrors are being committed. Someone is using egg whites to prepare floor polish. People's homes are being ransacked and children have no eggs to eat."

The short man picked up a fistful of almonds from the pile.

"Truly, all kinds of horrors are being committed. Hens are now trying to hatch pellets of dirt instead of eggs."

The holy man's eyes filled with tears but his disciple was not in the least moved.

"If the hens are warm and loving and persistent in their efforts, even pellets of dirt will give birth to chicks," he said.

The holy man looked at him and smiled. I turned to argue with the disciple.

"Pellets of dirt will never be transformed into chicks. For that you need an egg. It is true though that machines can be substituted for the hens."

The holy man turned to me and smiled again. The disciple and I continued to argue; neither of us was willing to concede. The short man sided with me and the tall man supported the disciple. What started as a verbal argument between the disciple and me turned into a fist fight between the two young men. With no resolution in sight, I turned to the holy man again and implored, "Oh, holy one, you who can see the past and the future, tell me what is happening here."

"What can he say?" said the disciple. "He has taken a vow of silence for a year. He will not speak."

The holy man turned to me and offered me a few cardamom pods.

"What am I supposed to do with these?" I asked the disciple.

"Pop them into your mouth and chew them, and you will soon forget about the eggs," he said and continued to massage the holy man's feet. The three of us got up and left.

"Now what?" I said to the short one.

"What?"

"I think we should go to the wise man," said the tall one. I agreed.

The short one did not come with us. He had to go and arrest a person who had been caught hiding ten eggs. The thief was to be hung from the bridge. The two of us, the tall one and I, went into an old house and started climbing up the stairs. I managed to go up four flights of steps fine but then started to breathe heavily. The tall man threw me over his shoulder and carried me up to the seventh floor. This was where the wise man lived.

The man was sitting at a table busy writing. In front of him was a cup of coffee. As the tall one put me down, I turned to the wise man and asked, "What are eggs for?"

"For eating of course, what else? Tell me would you like an omelet or an egg sandwich with your coffee?"

He reached into a drawer and pulled out two cups and a jar of coffee, planning to make some for us. But I put the cups back in the drawer and said, "I have not come here to drink coffee, I have come in search of an answer to a question."

"What is the question?" he asked.

"The question is if everyone has a right to eat eggs, how can one person be given the right to mix egg whites into the cement for his house?"

He gulped down his coffee, "That is not the fundamental question."

"Then what is the fundamental question?" I asked in surprise.

He took off his glasses, pulled out a handkerchief from his pocket and wiped his glasses clean before he put them on again.

"The fundamental question is which came first, the chicken or the egg." The tall one nodded his head vigorously.

"This question has received considerable attention," I said to the wise man, "but no one can say it is resolved."

"And that is why I am pondering over it," said the wise man as he started to scribble on a piece of paper.

"Do you think you will be able to resolve the question?"

"It is not necessary to resolve this question," he said. "Just considering it carefully is enough."

In frustration, I shouted, "Whether the egg came before or after is moot. The egg exists."

"What do you mean by existence?"

I had no response to this question. I was quiet. The tall man shook me.

"Are you asleep? Tell us what to exist means?"

The shaking woke me up. I had truly fallen into a stupor.

"You have seen an egg but have you ever been inside it?" the wise one asked, passing his hand over my head.

"Have you?" retorted the tall man on my behalf.

"But of course, why else would I say this." He took out the coffee jar and proceeded to make another cup. From the other drawer he took out a plate with an omelet on it.

Nibbling at his omelet and sipping his coffee, he spoke, "There was nothing there. Just a void. The same void that is inside you, inside me, inside him, inside this room, in the heavens and in the depths of hell."

I started to feel sleepy again. The tall man shook me awake and led me out of the room. The short man was waiting for us outside. His duty hours were over and he now wanted to hear what the wise man had to say.

"He didn't say anything," I responded. "Like the holy man, he too remained quiet."

Hearing this the tall man roared with laughter and turned to his companion and said, "The wise one answered in great detail. How would this man know? He was sleeping."

The short man started laughing too. Then one of them grabbed me by my right arm and tried to pull me to the right. The other caught hold of my left arm and pulled me to the left.

"He has to walk to the right. That is what's best for him," said one.

"No, he has to go left," said the other.

I pulled myself away from them, freed both my arms, clenched my fists, and ran away. I ran through alleys, bazaars, gardens, and farms until I reached a wide-open field. On the other side of the field were many colorful mansions that seemed to be hiding among the trees. Shiny new cars were parked in front. In the field itself were vast crowds of people, cowed with their heads inside their phĕrăns, silent as if they were dumbstruck. Their silence gnawed at me and I couldn't control myself.

"Why are you in despair?" I asked. "Only one of you has been hung from the bridge yet. Who knows how many more await that fate? Only three million eggs have been collected yet. I know you have handed over all the eggs you had. But these people believe that you are hiding many more. Your houses will be searched again today."

The crowd listened to me quietly. They did not respond or ask questions in return. I warmed to my subject.

"Don't you know how important eggs are for people? Eggs have protein and vitamins. Your features are pale because you have been denied eggs. And that is why you have lost your ability to speak. But today you need to make a decision. Take your heads out of your phĕrăns and revolt. If you do not rise up now you will be crushed. Listen to the horns of the cars across the field. If you stay quiet like this, these very cars will crush you."

I heard the sound of applause behind me, and turning around, I saw the tall man and the short man clapping vigorously. Without saying anything to either of them I continued with my speech.

"Why would we let anyone take our eggs away? These eggs are for eating, not for mixing with cement in construction work. I have no idea who is grabbing our eggs, but whoever he is we will not spare him."

I noticed the crowd getting restless. They were rising in twos and threes and, taking slips of paper from a man in white clothes and crossing to the other side of the field. In a few minutes the entire area was empty. I turned around and asked the two young men who the person in white was.

"That's him," said the short one.

"Who?" I asked, not comprehending.

"How come you don't understand anything easily," admonished the tall one.

His anger made me realize a few things, and I asked another question.

"Why was he passing out those slips of paper?"

"These are entry permits for the mansions," said the short one.

"What are these people going to do in those mansions?"

"We'll have to see," said the tall one.

They grabbed me and took me along with them. We entered a long corridor in one of the mansions. Here were the people who I had just been lecturing, lying flat on the ground, licking the floor with their tongues.

"What are they doing?" I asked.

"What do you think they are doing?" said the tall one. "The floor of this corridor has been constructed with the egg mixture in the cement. They're licking it in order to get the vitamins and proteins from the eggs into their bodies."

I observed the scene carefully. People were lying flat on their stomachs like upside down corpses. They were absolutely still, no part of their bodies, arms or legs were moving. Only their tongues were working steadily. The tongue would emerge, lick the floor and retreat back into the mouth. Only to emerge and lick the floor again. I continued to watch this scene until the man dressed in white came in. He swept his palm across a corner of the floor and turning to the tall one said, "Looks like the polish is good."

"Sir, there is no need for grinding machines now. We don't lack manpower in this country," the tall one remarked.

"And when the spit mixes with the egg, the polish takes on a different luster," offered the short one.

Then all three of them came outside. I stood alone in the hall and saw my reflection in the shining floor. The image was grotesque and I was frightened. Did I really look like that, I wondered? Or was the floor defective? But who could I ask? There were many people there but what could they say? Their tongues were busy licking the floor. There was silence all around. I debated whether I too should remain silent, but realized that between my friend and me, I alone had a voice. His tongue had been pulled from its roots, mine was still there. So how could I refrain from speaking? I decided to ask whoever I came across if my face was truly disfigured or was it the egg and spit-polished floor that was deceiving me?

A Late Winter

WHEN NOTHING IS STRAIGHTFORWARD, WHEN ALL PATHS
ARE crooked, when shaded places are covered with mounds
of snow and hollows become pools of water – at such moments
when you see a puddle on the right, you go left, but after just two
steps, you encounter another puddle and then you're trapped. You
cannot go forward nor can you turn back. When a vehicle blares its
horn, piercing not just your ears but also your heart, you are forced
to get out of the way in order to save your life. In trying to save your
life, you end up in a pool of water and spend the rest of the day nurs-
ing your frozen toes inside your drenched shoes and socks.

Their bus arrived in Srinagar the other day, at eleven-thirty at night.
As he was taking them home, the driver of the three-wheeler said,

"Bas jinab! We've had such stormy weather only since yesterday. It was a very pleasant winter here. There was an abundance of sunshine."

His wife heaved a long sigh when she heard this. But he remained unruffled. These past four years, they had left Kashmir every winter and come back only in the last few days of the fading season. Each year, when they returned, they would hear people say: "Jinab! This rain and snow started only recently. Before this the weather here was so warm that even the phěrǎn and kāngěr became a burden. The quilt covers we washed in the morning would be dry by the evening."

"If only you had extended your leave by ten, eleven days . . . What treasure did you hope to find here by returning so soon?"

He did not respond to his wife's remark; not because he did not have an answer. He had answers to many questions, but he kept them to himself. He would not let them out. He had come to realize that the answers he let out of his warm bosom into the open were not valued by anyone else. Once they were released, these beloved offspring of his mind wandered, dazed and adrift like orphans.

"Some questions have no answers," said his favorite son one Sunday while sunning himself on the balcony.

"There is an answer, but there is no question. The question has to be found."

"Do you think that if we looked, we could find it?"

He thought his son might be pulling his leg. He would often ask such seemingly innocent questions, perhaps just to exercise his father's aging mind, "Do you feel that if a person is so inclined, he can do anything he wants?"

"Do you believe that everything is changing?"

"Do you also accept that the truth is what we see, hear, or feel?"

He would often remain silent when faced with such questions.

That Sunday too, he was quiet. His son's attitude had changed after leaving home. He had started paying too much attention to trivial matters, who knows why?

Once on the footpath, he untied the lace of his left shoe and pulled his foot out. The shoe was not too damp inside. His socks though were a bit soiled near the ankle. It started drizzling. He looked around but could not find a safe corner that would shelter him. He opened his umbrella. He regained the confidence in himself that he had lost on many occasions in his encounters with rain and slush. While leaving home his wife had said, "Why are you taking this umbrella along? It isn't going to rain or snow anymore. You will just lose it!"

Somehow the things that his wife thought would happen never came to pass. She had thought that now her son had found work outside Kashmir, he would have a car to travel in, servants to serve him, and a big house to live in. But all he had was a pigeonhole of a room with a tiny balcony. The rent he paid for it took away a third of his salary. She had also thought that when she returned to Kashmir, almond trees, daffodils, and buttercups would have blossomed, collard greens and red spinach would have sprouted. But all she got was snow, cold, rain, and slush. She would wish for something, but what actually happened would be quite the opposite. And this would make her angry.

Today, again, she will be exasperated. She will tell him that he has soiled his clothes despite the umbrella.

His son, unlike his wife, neither aspired to anything nor lost his temper. He seemed to believe that nothing would change either by being hopeful or by becoming impatient. His son seemed at peace with himself. With no sign of desire or anger – he had turned into a robot of sorts.

But one day even this mechanical being came alive, exploded, and shook with rage. That day, his son and his daughter-in-law had both been insistent, "Why are the two of you suffocating in this dingy room? Go out, take a stroll. A wonderful South Indian temple has been built in the fourth sector. Go, visit it."

The bedroom of his son's apartment had a bathroom attached. He went in and came out after washing his hands and face. Meanwhile, his wife changed her sari, combed her hair and got ready to leave. They set off together to see the temple.

Unlike in Kashmir, where you have to move from inside to outside to accomplish certain tasks, in Delhi it is the opposite. Damn this prostate! It often troubles people after the age of fifty. He felt the need to go to the bathroom again. It wasn't hard to go to the bathroom. What was hard was that to do so, one had to go through the bedroom. The door was locked from the inside. He waited a while but after a bit, he was compelled to knock.

The door was opened, but somewhat grudgingly, it seemed. His son stood before him, his eyes bloodshot. The daughter-in-law had moved away to the balcony.

"I want to go to the bathroom."

"Didn't you just come out from there? You should get yourself treated."

After coming out, he sat on a chair to catch his breath. Then he turned to his son, "I intended to go for a thorough checkup at the Medical Institute this year. But you had no time to accompany me."

"You head for the Medical Institute even for trifles. Are there no doctors in Kashmir?"

"No, that's not the case. I thought since I was coming to Delhi anyway . . ."

"As though Delhi hasn't been kind enough to me already and all I need to accomplish here is to get your prostate fixed."

"What are you trying to say?"

"I am being honest. You destroyed my life by sending me here. I could have managed to get a job there! But no, you wouldn't let me look for one. You wanted to save yourselves from the winter cold over there and you wanted to bask in the sun here. You needed a place to stay."

He could not say a word, nor even stand up.

"Why are you sitting here? Why aren't you leaving? That poor woman is waiting for you outside!"

He couldn't hold himself back any longer. Across the road, an arcade of shops ended abruptly providing an opening. Ahead of him stood a cart parked in the middle of the road. Indeed, by placing his cart in the middle of the road, thus slowing down traffic and enabling pedestrians like him to walk across with relative ease, some ingenious fellow had fixed the problem that the city's municipality had failed to address. He practically ran across the road. His troubles left him for a bit as he started walking towards his home in a relaxed manner. But this state of calm did not last long. Recollecting the taunts of his wife and son, he grew agitated once again.

His wife was illiterate and stupid. But what was wrong with his son? Why doesn't he think? If one can't get a job done here, there is no reason why one can't cross over to the other side. and if that doesn't work out, one can always come back.

It had started raining hard. The umbrella saved his head and knees but the splashes from the ground drenched his pants. His gloveless hand that held the umbrella froze in the cold.

The grass should have already turned green. The buds in the trees should have already sprouted. The pale blue sky should have rent the cover of clouds and become clear. But the gloom of the clouds persisted as did the chill of the snow. The rain and slush are still around. This winter has dragged on too long.

But even then, how long could it last? Maybe another two, four or ten, twelve days . . .

"Do you still believe that in two, four, ten or fifteen days this miserable wintery weather will end?"

"No, not just *believe*, I know for sure! I will not stay quiet anymore when you taunt me. You are hundreds of miles away from me at the moment and I am still talking to you. This long winter will not last forever. I am not trying to sound sophisticated or clever, or trying to be deceptive or dramatic. What I've said is the plain, self-evident truth. People like you who waste a lot of mental energy on trivial stuff know this, so does your mother who does not pay attention to even the most pressing matters."

It had started snowing now, along with the rain. Suddenly, something went wrong with the umbrella. It shut like a cage over his head. He held it open with both hands – the handle of the umbrella with one hand and its ribs with the other – until he got home.

That Which We Cannot Speak Of

THEY SAY THAT LAL DĔD SPUN WOOL INTO EXTREMELY FINE threads but her mother-in-law was not impressed. Though a daughter-in-law is not entitled to be angry, this infuriated Lal. She threw the entire skein of thread into the lake and lotus stalks sprang from it. The fine, hair-like fibers that we see in lotus stalks are the same delicate threads spun by Lal. Maybe this is why, as a mark of reverence to Lal Dĕd, present-day writers and poets spin lofty tales or weave ideas as fragile as the fibers of the lotus stalk. But jinab! I am not one of those privileged writers and poets. My metabolism is weak. I can neither digest lotus stalks nor comprehend the subtlety of fine thread-like ideas. I can only eat simple collard greens and rice and understand, as they say in English, "the writing on the wall," inscribed in bold letters.

If you find what I just said too obscure, let me put it simply. There were sudden noises in the middle of the night. My wife thought it was the sound of gunfire or an exploding bomb. But I realized it was not a bomb, just the sound of firecrackers which suggested that Maqbool Sahib had won the assembly seat from our constituency. Usually my wife does not believe anything I say; but this time she was easily convinced. She again covered herself from head to foot with the blanket and went back to sleep. But I couldn't sleep and started thinking about the impact of Maqbool Sahib's victory on regional, national and international politics. I didn't get very far with that thought. Like a student in an examination hall who leaves a difficult question half done and moves on to an easier one, I started thinking about how Maqbool Sahib's victory would affect my life. This too wasn't as easy as I had thought at first. To answer such a question, one would need to be familiar with astrology. An astrologer well-versed in his profession can predict the good or bad impact of shifts in planetary alignments. I thought it better to put these theoretical concerns aside and focus on practical matters like when I might congratulate Maqbool Sahib and what I might say to him. Thinking about pointless abstractions made me lightheaded. But thinking about practical matters steadied my mind and led it back on track. As a result, before I could finalize a plan to visit Maqbool Sahib and congratulate him, I fell asleep once again.

My wife woke me at the crack of dawn.

"Hey you! Maqbool Sahib may have won the election, but you won't get collard greens later."

Why wouldn't I get the collard greens? Collard greens are perhaps the only thing available in Kashmir all through the year. Since the beginning of life in Kashmir, people have asked God to bless them with rice and collard greens. Though rice became scarce, collard greens were always abundant. Actually, my wife meant that if I were late, I would miss the famous Kawdor collard greens that the red-haired street vendor sold which, in my wife's opinion, were delicious.

Heavy-eyed, I picked up the bag and left for the market. Only Magga's, that is Mohammad Maqbool's, barber's shop was open. Apart from him, Nazir Woin, Basheer Goor, his younger brother Farooq and Rahman Gaad'e were standing in front of the shop. Rahman Gaad'e was going on about how even though the counting of votes had been completed the same day, the officials were hesitant to announce the results. Just then Magga saw me and yelled, "Today the rascals look disgraced."

I was not angry when I heard Magga say this. Why would I be angry? I didn't feel disgraced. My face was unwashed, perhaps that made me look somewhat dejected. Only those who have time and leisure can afford to feel outraged. I was in a hurry and if I were late by even a minute, I would miss those special collard greens from Kawdor that taste better than ghee.

The vegetable seller sold sixteen bunches of collard greens for a rupee. I got three more by haggling and another four by tricking him. On my way home I bumped into Magga near his shop, or who knows, maybe he purposely bumped into me. I can't say for sure. As

I was about to fall into the gutter Magga shouted out loud, *"Batta, are you blind?"*

Whether or not I could see clearly before, I felt completely blind after he yelled at me. Only God knows how I managed to get back home. If you poke a bull, it goes into a frenzy. On the contrary if you insult a Batta by calling him a Batta, he gets really frightened.

The day before yesterday, someone from our family had been traveling to Jammu. Six or seven of us packed ourselves into a taxi like sardines and set off for the tourist center. The taxi driver was irritated but did not react. When he started the taxi, I told him politely,

"Brother, you forgot to turn the meter on."

As soon as I said this, he stopped the car, got out and started shouting, "Damn you, Batta! It'll cost you thirty rupees, that's final! Otherwise get out. Don't pollute my car."

I flinched. Struggling to smile, I said, "Sir, don't be so angry early in the morning. You're not a stranger, you're like my brother. Charge thirty-one instead of thirty!"

After reaching the tourist center and paying him thirty rupees, I found out that he too was a Batta. I clenched my fists, but there was nothing I could do about it now. Had I known this fifteen minutes earlier I would have shouted him down, saying, "Damn you, cowardly Batta! Will you turn the on meter or should I teach you a lesson?"

And he would have tried to pacify me: "Sir, don't be furious. Look here, I have turned the meter on, and now, you can pay me a rupee less than what it shows."

I unleashed the anger I felt towards Magga on my wife as soon as I got home. I flung the collard greens at her and went straight up to my room. I lit a cigarette and started thinking about what was wrong with Magga. It was Maqbool Sahib who had won, not Magga and it was Doctor Janaki Nath Koul who had lost, not I. In a way, I was closer to Maqbool Sahib than to Doctor Janaki Nath. He and I had taught together in the same college for six years. Besides this, Magga's anger would have made sense only if Maqbool Sahib had lost the election, it would be justified if Maqbool Sahib had fallen short of votes because of my family and myself. Success and failure are both in the hands of God. Only those whom God wishes to save recover from illness. Doctors and hakeems are only His instruments. So also, only the candidate whom God favors wins an election. The voter is just a medium. They are ineffectual. Even if the voter wishes you ill, all that matters is God's will!

Maqbool Sahib was my colleague, but Magga was no stranger either. He was my schoolmate. We studied together from Class I to Class V in the Shitty School. Formally the school was named Government Primary School, but people called it Compulsory School, Compulsory Rag School or Shitty School. It was called Shitty School because the spot where it had been built had once been a public lavatory. To turn a lavatory into a school was a noble deed that could only have been accomplished in our neighborhood. Although, these days the stench that emanates from our education system makes one think that all schools and colleges have been built on sites which were previously lavatories.

Magga and I studied together in this Shitty School until Class

V. Then my father sent me to high school, then college, and then to university. Later I got a job and was married off. Magga dropped out from school after Class V. After leaving Shitty School, he played hopscotch and marbles and gambled right outside the school compound. Then he disappeared for some time, only to appear again when I was taking the Class X examinations. He got married and soon after his father passed away, Magga took his father's place at the barber's shop and started cutting people's hair. In the beginning, I too would go to his shop for a haircut. He charged me less than he did the other customers in acknowledgement of our childhood friendship. But Magga had revised his rates ever since inflation had ruined the economy over the past ten to twelve years. He charged other customers two or three rupees but took only one rupee from me. But still, I'd stopped going to his shop. Five years ago, Magga's younger half-brother also opened a barber's shop in our neighborhood. Now I go to his shop for a haircut. He charges me five rupees. No sir, I didn't have a quarrel with Magga nor did I think his half-brother was a better barber. I have been smoking cigarettes for twenty-four years now and have gone to the barber's for almost twice that long, but I never found one cigarette brand better or worse than the other. And I could never distinguish a master barber from a novice. Why I abandoned Magga and went to his half-brother's shop is something that cannot be talked about. You may well question the veracity of everything I have said so far. You are right, why should I hide this one fact? There was only a fifteen-year-old calendar and three photographs hanging on the walls in Magga's shop. On the calendar was a small, beautiful child dressed for Eid with a Koran in front of him and his hands held up in prayer. There was a photograph of Sheikh Abdullah, another photograph of Magga's father, and a third one of Magga with his three friends. In contrast, all the walls in his half-brother's shop were covered with pictures of film actresses and other stunning women. Their faces were alluring and their hips, thighs, and other parts were even more attractive. As I waited about thirty or forty minutes for my turn, I would dedicate about five minutes to each picture, and this brought peace and tranquility to my soul. When I would leave the shop after the haircut both my head and mind felt lighter. The younger generation of women in my family also read magazines and books with similar pictures but they did so in secret.

This was the real reason I went to his brother's shop. But Magga believed I had abandoned him over political disagreements. He thought I had stopped going to his shop and quit our old social circle because I was in league with his half-brother. The truth is that the reason for our differences was not the photograph of Sheikh Abdullah hanging on the wall of his shop, nor the blowup of Hema Malini pasted on the wall of his half-brother's. The real reason for the break in our friendship was indeed a photograph, but that photograph was of Beigh Sahib. It's a fact that Sheikh Sahib's photograph hangs in Magga's shop even today, but Beigh Sahib's photograph was destroyed even before it could be developed from the roll of film. A photograph may or may not survive but its story lives on.

Some years ago, a group of boys went to Sonerwani for a picnic. We arrived at the Manasbal Lake at nine-thirty in the morning, and the boys decided to have tea there before going further. By sheer luck, the Pride of Kashmir, Mirza Muhammad Afzal Beigh, was staying at the local guest house at that time. Maqbool Sahib and I held back but the boys formed a circle around Beigh Sahib. In those days the state police had arrested many young men on allegations of conspiring to break up the Indian Union. Beigh Sahib was fighting for them in court and had come to Manasbal to prepare his case. After about ten minutes some of our boys came up to us and asked if they could take a photograph with Beigh Sahib. Maqbool Sahib looked at me and asked me what I thought. But what could I say, I told him to do whatever he thought appropriate. But the boys did not wait for our consent. They made Beigh Sahib sit on a chair and stood around him. One boy went up to take the photograph. As he was about to click the button, Beigh Sahib shouted, "Professors, why don't you join us. No one will fire you from your jobs over this."

Maqbool Sahib was annoyed with me. He said, "I told you we should drive straight to Sonerwani. Now go and get your picture taken. You will realize how serious this is when this picture is published in the newspaper tomorrow. But you have nothing to worry about, you are a Batta. No one will hold you accountable but I'll be in trouble."

Maqbool Sahib was right, but perhaps not entirely. I still haven't forgotten that winter day, before I married and was appointed a college lecturer. I was an ordinary employee in a government office and was friends with the lovely Shanta, the daughter of a poor widow, who lived in our neighborhood. I remember vividly, it was a Friday. Sheikh Sahib had been released from jail a few days before and was going to the dargah to deliver a lecture. But none of this affected me. I left for the office as usual at ten o'clock in the morning and Shanta told her mother that she was going to visit a friend. We met at the Habba Kadal Bridge. At first, we thought we might watch a movie but then realized our families might see us at Ameera Kadal. We walked along the banks of Dood Ganga till Chattabal and kept walking until we reached Shalteng. We came back at four o'clock. The next day when I went to the office, I was asked to explain my absence. The government had issued a circular that action would be taken against those government employees who had not come to work but had gone instead to Sheikh Sahib's lecture at the Dargah. My boss, a low-ranking officer then, and now a senior official who is a thorn in the side of the powers in Delhi – was quick to reprimand me. He swore at me, calling me an American and a Pakistani agent, and then he suspended me. My family and I were distressed and Shanta was the only one who supported me at that time. A compounder named Mohammad Maqbool, who had started a pharmacy near her mother's house, asked someone to call my boss and intervene. I was given my job back. Batta got his job back – and a government job at that! It was like a blind man regaining his sight. Shanta was so impressed with the Mohammad Maqbool's compassion that a few days later she eloped with him and till today, no one knows anything about their whereabouts. Excuse me for this digression, please . . .

I was talking about Beigh Sahib. Beigh Sahib did not wait for Maqbool Sahib's reply or mine. He asked the guard to fetch two more chairs and the two of us sat on either side of him with the boys standing around. Helplessly, we posed for the photograph.

On the bus ride from Manasbal to Sonerwani, Maqbool Sahib didn't speak a word to me. He sighed once and said, "Now no one can save us except the Almighty."

And sure enough, the Almighty came to our rescue. At Sonerwani, the boy who had taken the photograph came to us and said, "We want to sit on those rocks. The camera might slip and fall in the water, so could you please keep it with you?"

"Yes," Maqbool Sahib responded immediately, as if he had been waiting for that very moment. As soon as the boy went away, Maqbool Sahib opened the camera, took out the roll of film and exposed it. He then rolled the film again and inserted it back into the camera. He seemed relieved but he remained annoyed with me. He swore and said that associating with a naïve person like me was to strangle oneself. Five or six days later we learned that a group of our college boys had vandalized a photographer's shop for selling them an expired roll of film.

As I was recalling these events, I forgot to shave, wash up, or have tea. A true Batta can forget everything but he won't forget to get to work. I sprang up at nine-thirty, shaved, washed my face quickly, ate a plateful of rice with collard greens, wore my suit and tie and left for college. Once again, I noticed Magga talking to some people in front of his shop. The moment he saw me, he said loudly, "The other day

Maqbool Sahib said in public that anyone living here under Delhi's patronage must leave; Kashmir isn't anyone's personal property."

"Hey Magga, in 1946 their own Nehru told them to either assimilate, run away or perish," Rahman Gaad'e added.

"God willing we will smoke these rats out. Wait and see," Magga sneered.

"But we won't let them take their women. We will keep their women here," Nazir Woin laughed loudly.

I thought it best to keep quiet. I lowered my head and continued walking. Gir Gagur was raising the shutters of his shop. He spoke sharply to Magga and his friends: "What's wrong with you guys? You should be ashamed of using such foul language in front of Professor Sahib."

Gir Gagur's words eased my discomfort somewhat. I waited there until he had opened his shop and then bought a pack of cigarettes. He whispered into my ear as he returned my change, "You should ignore them. They are too many to fight."

"That's what I did. They started swearing at me. I was just going to college."

"Why the hell did you take this route? You could have gone the other way, taken a ferry across the river straight to your college," he said.

Gir Gagur's advice was worth considering. I decided to take the other route and the ferry across the river to reach my college from now on. It would cost me fifty paisa there and back but that would not kill me.

At college, I was anxious, wondering if everything at home

was all right. I was worried that someone might harass my wife. I reached home earlier than usual, at three o'clock, and found her cheerful, dressed up and ready to go out.

"Where are you going?" I asked.

"Don't you remember we have to go to Buchpora today," she said. "How forgetful you have become!"

I remembered then that Jawe Lal, a relative of mine who lived in Ganpatyaar, was getting his daughter married. The groom's family had told them that there would be wealthy guests accompanying the groom and they could not bring the wedding procession to that seedy Ganpatyaar neighborhood. Poor Jawe Lal was very agitated. Many of his relatives lived in posh areas like Karan Nagar, Jawahar Nagar, Channapora, and Shivpora but none of their homes were available for the wedding ceremony. Jawe Lal had discussed this problem with a colleague, Maqbool Hussain Mir, who had recently built a house in Buchpora. He said to Jawe Lal, "Your daughter is like my own. If my house cannot be of help now, it is of no use."

The wedding was still a few days away and since it was a daughter getting married, we had to ask Jawe Lal if he needed anything.

The bus was very crowded. There was barely room to stand, let alone sit down. Eventually, a young man took pity on my wife and said to her, "Hey, Congress lady, come, sit here on the bonnet."

Today, he called her a Congress lady, six years back, another man had addressed her as "Janta lady," and before that she was called a "grand lady." The labels Congress, Janta, or grand did not matter, what matters is the word "lady." It is almost like a refrain in a poem.

While the lines change, the refrain stays the same. She is always a "lady."

We reached Buchpora at seven in the evening. My wife started chatting with Jawe Lal's and Mir Sahib's wives in the kitchen while I went to the drawing room. Jawe Lal and his friend Mir Sahib, the owner of the house, were not there, but a few people from Jawe Lal's family were. I sat in a corner. There was a priest there whom I did not know. He looked at me for a while and then asked Jawe Lal's cousin, "Kishen Ji, tell me, is the kitchen clean?"

"Yes, it's clean," he replied.

The priest then got to the crux of the matter. "In my opinion, Jawe Lal has made a mistake. How can sacred wedding rituals like Kanyadan and Brahma Yagna be performed in a mleccha's house? Would this be sanctioned by the Vedas and other holy books?

"The groom's mother is also upset. She has expressed that sending the groom to a Muslim's house is inauspicious," Kishen Ji responded.

"She's right, bless her," Pandit remarked and turned to me, "Could you shut the door, please. Sometimes one wishes to have a private conversation but how is that possible when these people are everywhere." I closed the door, and he continued speaking. "Give them half a chance and they'll slaughter us all in an instant. I don't know what's stopping them.

"They used to restrain themselves out of courtesy but not anymore," Kishen Ji added his opinion.

At that moment, the door was flung open and Mir Sahib entered the room. We all greeted him. He offered us some tea; we replied that we'd had tea in our homes. He ignored our response and insisted that we must have something. He told us that Jawe Lal would be back soon, the groom's family had brought up a few problems and he had gone to speak to the matchmaker.

With Mir Sahib's arrival, the subject of our conversation changed. Pandit Ji praised the locality. Kishen Ji added, "Battas are cowards. They have moved to far-flung areas like Pampore and Khrew but they never considered moving here. As if they would be killed."

An animated political discussion followed these remarks, then moved on to the recent elections and we had soon formed a cabinet of finance, power, industry, forest, and health ministries.

I asked if anyone knew who would get the Education ministry.

"Education will go to Maqbool Sahib. He has been a professor and is the most suitable candidate," Kishen Ji replied.

This made me uneasy, as if I was sitting on pins. My wife and I left without waiting for Jawe Lal to return. I couldn't sleep a wink that night. In the morning, I got up, shaved, took a bath and left for Maqbool Sahib's house without having my tea. He was pleased to see me and seemed to have forgotten our old disagreement. I congratulated him on the win; he thanked me. I said that actually it is the people of our constituency who deserve praise for electing a scholar and setting such an admirable precedent. He said that he would only be able to achieve something great if he had the support of progressive, secular intellectuals like me; people who weren't narrow-minded or partisan in their views. He served me tea, and before I left, he mentioned that his son, Munna, was going to appear for the Class XII examination. I told him that I would probably be setting one of the mathematics papers for this year. He said that was great news. I remarked that I would come to see him at a suitable time. He replied that he wasn't worried about that. He wanted to send Munna to IIT Delhi for his college degree and I told him it would be a little difficult to get admission there. He said he knew some people who could help, but if Munna scored well in the exams, it would be easier.

I left half an hour later, after the conversation with Maqbool Sahib was over. As I stepped outside, I saw Magga and a few men at the door. The guard would not let them in to the house. He had told them that Maqbool Sahib was busy discussing some important matters with an influential political leader.

When Magga saw me coming out, he became very angry. He pushed the guard aside and charged in. But before going inside, he shouted, "Is this idiot Batta the influential political leader you were talking about?"

He said other things too, which I didn't hear. I left like a rat smoked out of its hiding place. I thought to myself that while it's great to be friends with Maqbool Sahib, in the end, I have to live in the same neighborhood as Magga. I should make peace with him. But how? I pondered this for a while and arrived at a solution. I realized that I had to renounce my feelings for Hema Malini and Parveen Babi and go back to Magga's shop for a haircut. His resentment was sure to vanish. But I was also apprehensive, just like the Battas who were terrorized in 1931 when their homes and shops were looted in

Vecharnag and Maharajgunj. They were astonished when they realized that Muslims were in control of everything. From midwives to cemetery workers, and from carpenter's tools to barber's razors, everything was in their hands. Midwives, cemetery workers, and carpenters might be harmless, but a barber could easily slit a Batta's jugular while shaving, and the poor fellow would die in a second. They say that this was what compelled some Batta boys to give up the proscriptions and become barbers. The throats of the old Battas remained safe, but those young boys were unable to find girls to marry. No respectable Batta would marry his daughter to a barber.

Jinab, forgive me. I've committed another blunder, I shouldn't have told you this story. If I continue talking, I will commit many more blunders. Let me leave this here.

The News

IT IS DIFFICULT FOR ME TO SAY WHETHER SHE ACTUALLY KNOCKED on the door or it only appeared that she had. I got out of bed, quickly put on my clothes, opened the door, and went out. She was standing right there. She didn't say a word, nor did I ask any questions. The situation had already moved beyond the point of conversation. Everything was clear and evident now. I had prepared myself for this since the previous evening.

I gestured with my head and followed her to the small room where a lamp was lit. In its dim light I saw that Băb's lifeless body had been brought down from the bed and placed on the floor. His eyes were closed. But his mouth, kept tightly shut for so many years, was now open. I felt the urge to do or say something but I could neither act nor come up with any appropriate words. Suddenly a thought occurred to me, and I said to her: "We should place the lamp near Băb's pillow." Considering that this was, perhaps, the right thing to do at a time like this, she did as I suggested.

"His mouth is open," she declared.

"Why shouldn't it be? He must have finally opened his mouth to utter what we have been waiting to hear all these years – the matter that he never found the courage to speak of," I said, expressing what I believed.

She disagreed, "No, that is not what it is. Băb is waiting for them. He will not close his mouth until they come and give him the final sip of water." I had not thought that this could be a possible reason for Băb's open mouth, but I held on to the idea. Actually, I was looking for an excuse to get out of there. I left her alone with the corpse in that dingy room and went to give the news of Băb's death to those people who, according to her, he was waiting for with his mouth wide open.

All the roads seemed deserted in the dark, there was not a soul in sight, not even a glimpse of the trees that line the roads. It was as if the cold and darkness had devoured everything. The stray dogs too, the ones that roamed through the streets all day, seemed to have vanished. It was so cold that water from the dripping taps along the road had frozen into icicles. I was glad I had not cried upon seeing Băb's dead body. Had I wept, my tears would have turned into icicles too, blurring my vision. Because I hadn't wept, my vision was clear and sharp. It pierced through the veil of darkness, looked past the doors and windows, and revealed naked sleeping bodies lying comfortably in soft, warm beds. To sleep without a care in cozy beds, not worrying about death, is the greatest luxury one can wish for. At that time, I wondered what had deprived me of this pleasure . . . and realized that it was my own doing.

I had volunteered to inform the people about Băb's death. Or rather, I had created an excuse to run away from the dead body with its mouth open in that dimly lit room.

I was familiar with the house to which I was going to deliver the news; it was at the far end of the road. But after taking only a few strides, I was confused. The road I knew to be straight had branched into two. What should I do? Which road should I take? Eventually, I decided like anyone in my situation would have. I resolved to take the one on the right first. If it led me to my destination, I was there. Otherwise, I would turn back and take the one on the left. This plan would obviously take more time, but it is better to arrive late than never. But there was more to it: long roads are easier to traverse than long nights. Wandering the roads might somehow bring this night to an end.

The man of the house, his wife and their son were all pleased to see me, their happiness evident in their radiant smiles. But my mouth was shut and my face distorted.

Their living room was brightly lit. The heat inside had turned it into a hammam. I felt as if I had found the light and warmth I had craved for so long.

A large portrait of Băb hung on one of the walls. As soon as I looked at it, the man said, "Whoever comes here turns to Băb's portrait first and bows in front of it before sitting down." But I sat down against a pillow without making any such gesture. Soon his wife entered with tea and sweets. It seemed improper to eat at such a somber moment. But she insisted I take some in Băb's name, "You cannot refuse."

"Whatever I am and whatever I have – my house, my wife, my son – I owe it all to Băb. We owe him our very existence," said the man. He held the plate of sweets in his hand and forced me to take one while he put a big piece in his own mouth. It felt like I was sipping poison, not tea. I didn't know how to broach the sad news of Băb's death. How could I deliver the devastating news that would bring gloom to a happy family?

Appropriate or not, a messenger has to deliver the news.

Done with the tea, I got up quietly and turned Băb's portrait around to face the wall. "Băb has left us; this is a terrible blow." I said, in order to explain what I had just done.

"Băb does not abandon people. He comes himself to lift those who have fallen, no matter where he is." The man smiled as he turned Băb's picture around again.

Unable to restrain myself, I announced, "Băb is dead!"

The man grew angry. He grabbed me by my throat and shouted, "You bearer of bad news! Don't utter these inauspicious words in front of me! I will kill you!"

I ran out of there as quickly as I could, but I felt as if he were chasing me.

"Have you come back alone?" She sprang up when she saw me.

I went straight to the room and stood beside the body. "Did they get the news?" she asked.

I didn't say anything. When I entered, I started to feel suffocated again. I wanted to grab her hand, pull her to my room, and free her from the sight of the withered body in that dimly lit room. Secure in our cozy bed, we would stay there until the foul smell from that insect-ridden, rotting body would carry the news of its death to the whole world.

This is what I would have liked to do. But at the moment, there was nobody in that icy, dark, dingy room other than the two of us. And yes, between us was a frozen, withered body with its eyes shut and its mouth open.

Dogs

I LOOKED AT A PLEASANT DISPLAY OF FLOWER BEDS AND AN EVEN more attractive velvety green lawn adorned by the flowers. In the middle of this lush greenery, and under the shade of Chinar trees, stood a beautiful row of houses. Windowpanes that glistened in the sun, with soft muslin curtains on the inside that flowed like waterfalls. Through the curtains, beautiful women could be glimpsed every now and then like flashes of lightning.

I was so mesmerized that I forgot why I was there. I must confess to my lack of sophistication: this world of flowers, shady trees, verdant lawns, sparkling clear windowpanes and soft muslin curtains felt more like a picnic spot, a sanctuary, than a bustling residential neighborhood.

In contrast, the image of home carved in my heart from my

childhood was one of ugly bricks and ungainly, irregular wooden beams. Smoke-darkened ceilings and mud-plastered walls, rooms full of broken trunks and torn clothes, an empty sun-scorched yard. I still remembered how, during the Pann festival, my mother would give each one of us some rice husk and grass stalks to hold in our hands. After hearing her tell the story of Pann, we would throw those bits of rice and grass into the ritual vessel. On those mornings, I would leave early for Dewan Bagh or Gole Bagh in search of green and dried grass, because there was no hint of greenery in any of the yards where I lived. In all these years, and even as the tradition of observing the Pann festival has died out, not even a weed has grown in our neighborhood.

I shook my head vigorously, freed myself from the vision of those smoke-darkened, junk-filled rooms, and looked around the place I was standing in. This was the residential area of the university, and here, in house number 27-A, lived Dr. Siddiqui. While leaving home today, I had thought carefully about what I wanted to say to him. He had moved here, barely three months ago, as the head of the department of chemistry. In those three months, I had visited him several times. However, I had always left without saying what was on my mind, but not before having a cup of tea. But today I was determined to ask him if I could get a job as a lecturer in his department. After all, with a PhD in Chemistry I wasn't resigned to be a schoolteacher for the rest of my life.

I knew Dr. Siddiqui from when I had been a research scholar at Lucknow University. He was a junior faculty member in the chemistry department there. My own thesis advisor was Dr. Nagpal, who was very good friends with Dr. Siddiqui. People around us often referred to them as brothers. Back in January 1957, when protests against the then head of department, Professor Rajan, were being organized, it was rumored that the posters which had sprung up overnight all over campus had been drafted by Dr. Siddiqui and Dr. Nagpal. Recently I had requested a letter of recommendation addressed to Dr. Siddiqui from Dr. Nagpal, but God knows whether that letter will ever get here. Now I was determined to talk to Dr. Siddiqui about my problems directly.

As soon as I rang the bell to 27-A, the door swung open and Mrs. Siddiqui came out of the house with her black dog. She was delighted to see me and walked back into the house, pulling Shadow, the dog, behind her. I glanced at my watch and realized that this was the time for Shadow's daily walk. I tried to persuade Mrs. Siddiqui that she shouldn't change her routine because of me. She should take Shadow for a walk, I suggested, and I would pop in and say hello to Dr. Siddiqui.

She laughed and said that she had her entire life to walk Shadow. Besides, Dr. Siddiqui was not home. He had left a little while earlier to meet the vice chancellor. "Why don't the two of us sit together for a while and talk like old times?" she offered.

I certainly did not object to this and followed her inside. I had known Mrs. Siddiqui previously as well. Even before I had met Dr. Siddiqui.

I knew her then as Archana Verma. She had been a fellow research student in the chemistry department in Lucknow. A talented girl from a well-to-do family in Gorakhpur. She was tall, and when dressed in her starched handloom saris and blouses, she exuded a certain sensuality. But more than everything else, I liked her dusky face, particularly her dark full lips that glistened like jewels. Those luscious lips always reminded me of the juicy blackberries of my childhood. I confess that I often fantasized about tasting those lips just to see if they were truly as sweet and juicy as those blackberries.

In those days, I used to work under Dr. Nagpal while Archana worked with Dr. Siddiqui. It took me three years to submit my dissertation and another six months to get my degree. But Archana was a quick study. Within a year and half, she had married Dr. Siddiqui, and their daughter Daisy was born less than a year after. Her PhD was set aside. Daisy is older now. Mrs. Siddiqui does not worry about her daughter anymore. The last time I was here, both husband and wife told me that she intended to start her research project again.

Mrs. Siddiqui accompanied me to the drawing room, and after I sat down, she went to the kitchen to make some tea. She let go of the leash and left the dog behind. There is a certain kind of dog – small, white and fluffy like a cotton ball – that you want to pick up, sit on your lap and stroke. But Shadow was a different breed. He was black as coal, with short legs and a long body. All humans and animals are either short or tall. But I could never figure out whether to think of Shadow as short or long. Perhaps he had a fancy pedigree, but I only saw him as a little dog. For me, it was a matter of immense distress that the two of us, the dog and I, were staring at each other in the same room where I would often discuss matters of great intellectual importance with Dr. Siddiqui. While the dog just glared at me or sniffed at other objects from across the room, I sat quietly. But when he started to prowl around my legs, I let out a sharp cry. This brought Daisy running into the room, and catching hold of Shadow's leash, she pulled him back.

"He doesn't bite," she said in English.

"Well then, it's my fault. Perhaps he was just trying to hug me," I responded in English as well, and Daisy and I both laughed.

"Shadow is not badly behaved," continued Daisy. "Until a month ago, he had a trainer who taught him proper manners for an hour every day. And for this, my father paid him three hundred rupees every month," she said.

This remark really surprised me. I tutored two students for an hour and half every day. But they only paid me two hundred rupees each. Perhaps it was harder to train a dog than a human, hence the higher compensation, I reasoned.

Mrs. Siddiqui came back into the room with tea and biscuits. Shadow went into a frenzy when he saw the biscuits. Either he was hungry, or this was just normal behavior for a dog of his breed when it saw food. I thought he would attack the plate of biscuits and finish them off in one swoop. But the training he had received stood him in good stead. Despite his hunger and frenzy, he stood by quietly as Daisy picked up a biscuit and threw it on the floor. Shadow raced across the room and stood next to the dropped biscuit but did not eat it. He looked beseechingly at Daisy and her mother, who were both laughing. I could not understand why they were laughing. Soon, Daisy ordered Shadow to 'eat' in English and the dog fell upon the biscuit.

I was startled at first, then pleased, and completely in awe of the dog trainer's competence. Why charge just three hundred rupees a month? In my opinion, the trainer deserved at least five hundred. The better the doctor or the tutor, the more he should be compensated. My colleagues tutor groups of students and charge them a hundred and fifty rupees each. I just charge seventy-five rupees for group classes and two hundred rupees to tutor individually at home. That's why I can only open my students' eyes, but I cannot make them see.

While drinking my tea, I learned that Dr. Siddiqui had gone to the vice chancellor's office to resolve a particularly vexing issue. He was unlikely to return home before nine o'clock. Mrs. Siddiqui asked if I had any particular reason to visit. At that very moment, I forgot why I had come there.

"No, I just dropped by to say hello, nothing more," I said.

"That's good. Then forget that you had come to meet Dr. Siddiqui, the head of the chemistry department. Pretend that you came to meet an old classmate, Archana Verma," she replied.

I laughed, and it would have been easy for her to infer many things from my laughter. Daisy, along with Shadow, had left the room by now and I could talk without hesitation. I turned to her and said, "Please don't be upset, but honestly, despite his breeding and training, I still don't like Shadow."

She opened her large eyes wide in astonishment, and I was instantly reminded of the old Archana Verma of my Lucknow University days. I went on to propose that our affection for a person didn't depend on their appearance – we looked at their character, their education and background – but as far as dogs were concerned, appearances were critical.

I immediately realized that this was, perhaps, not the best way to communicate my theories. I hoped that she would not think I was comparing Dr. Siddiqui and Shadow. Mrs. Siddiqui was certainly dusky in appearance, but she did not have the coal-black skin tone that Dr. Siddiqui had. Her face was the color of brown winter blankets, with lips the color of blackberries. Dr. Siddiqui's face was ebony black, with lips that looked like burnt coal. In fact, Dr. Siddiqui and Shadow were almost identical as far as their colouring went. I tried to change the subject and jokingly suggested that perhaps Dr. Siddiqui, using all his knowledge of chemistry, had created Shadow in his laboratory.

But Mrs. Siddiqui did not support me in my attempts to find humor in this suggestion. "Dr. Siddiqui did not acquire Shadow," she said gravely. "I brought him home and nursed him. My husband, too, did not initially take to Shadow."

"Do you have a certain attraction for the color black," I blurted out, then realized that she might misinterpret that too as a reference to Dr. Siddiqui.

But she paid no attention to my remarks and said that she had a very strong belief in astrology and horoscopes. Surreptitiously, she had had Daisy's horoscope made right after the girl's birth. Six months ago, a senior astrologer from Varanasi had read both her own and Daisy's horoscopes. He had advised her that a black dog would bring good fortune to the family. Coincidentally, Dr. Siddiqui had to go to Delhi for a seminar around that time and Archana accompanied him. With the help of a friend, she had acquired Shadow in Delhi. Dr. Siddiqui had been very upset. Not just with the dog, but also with the reason behind his adoption. He had lamented the fact that, despite Archana's marriage to him, a scientist, she was not able to walk away from superstitious beliefs that were centuries old. But when, within a month of Shadow's arrival, Dr. Siddiqui was made the head of department, he began to believe that the dog was indeed lucky for them. And now, he was more solicitous of Shadow than even Daisy or her mother. When they returned to Kashmir, Dr. Siddiqui made arrangements to hire a dog trainer with the help of a friend in the army. Now, he would walk the dog himself all the way to the end of Naseem Bagh every morning. While Dr. Siddiqui was happy to eat just vegetables for days on end, Shadow had to be fed meat, kidneys, tripe, and all kinds of delicacies.

After an hour or so, I got up to leave. Mrs. Siddiqui accompanied me outside. She took Shadow's leash from Daisy, and still talking, she and the dog walked me to the bus stop. The bus appeared to be waiting just for me, because it started to move as soon as I stepped into it. I looked back and energetically waved goodbye to Mrs. Siddiqui. And then, as if out of nowhere, a pack of street dogs appeared and attacked Shadow. I did not witness what transpired, but I did hear later that Shadow had been badly mauled. I confess that I am spiteful, and this news made me happy.

The Lights on the Other Side

Nath Ji and Pyari were watching folk songs on television
– watching rather than listening. They kept the volume very
low. All of a sudden, a series of sounds startled them. The pressure
cooker in the kitchen shrieked, and the outer door shut with a bang.
Pyari got up and lowered the flame of the gas stove in the kitchen.
Nath Ji waited a moment, but when nobody called out or climbed up
the stairs, he stood up as well.

"Where are you going?" Pyari asked as she came back from the
kitchen.

"There was a noise at the door downstairs, but nobody came up."

"If someone was at the door, they would have come up. Relax."

But Nath Ji did·not sit down. He shuffled towards the window.
This annoyed Pyari further and she muttered to herself, "Let him

hang around the window forever. As if people have nothing better to do than show up and chat!" She raised the volume of the television. Rather than playing their instruments, the singers seemed to be beating their chests, swinging their heads and singing at the tops of their voices: "Either he will slay me with a dagger, or stay here for the night!"

Nath Ji opened the window. The twilight had just about faded. He could not see anything. But the door had made a sound. Or was it his imagination? Again, he thought of Gullĕ Chān, the carpenter, who had not fixed the clasp and the spring on the door properly. If one touched the door lightly from outside, it would open on its own and then slam shut. Maybe this time, too, someone had pushed it intentionally, just to annoy Nath Ji.

Nath Ji glanced at the unpaved road outside and then at the main road that it merged with. Across the road, willow trees stretched as far as the eye could see – some on dry land and some partially submerged in water. Beyond these willow groves, there was still another road and an embankment along the river. Across the river was the highway and, next to it, in the foothills, a military hospital, a canteen, and rows upon rows of army officers' quarters. But these unpaved and paved roads, these willows and so on were visible only in the daylight. At this moment, in the dark, they were indistinguishable from each other. Only the electric lights in the army quarters built on higher ground were visible, appearing like a lightshow across this sea of darkness.

"Is there anyone outside?" Pyari asked. Nath Ji shook his head. "Then why don't you shut the window? It's getting cold in here!"

But Nath Ji did not shut the window. He turned towards his wife, "Have you noticed the beautiful view from here in the evenings? Far across the river, the lights in the army quarters look like Bombay at night."

"When were you ever in Bombay that you'd know?" Pyari asked derisively.

"I never said I've been to Bombay. Maybe I saw something similar in a film or imagined that Marine Drive would look as beautiful as this at night."

"He begged you to visit last winter and the one before, didn't he? You should have gone," Pyari said softly.

Nath Ji shut the window and sat in his usual place. He stayed quiet for a while and then responded to Pyari's question with a question of his own: "How could I have gone? I have to repay a thousand rupees every month on the loan for this place and I tutor more students in the winter. And who would have looked after the house?"

"Well, this year we have a tenant downstairs."

"Yes, sure. But only this year," Nath Ji sighed.

Pyari felt uneasy. She went to the kitchen. Meanwhile, Nath Ji quietly pulled an atlas out from under the books. He opened it and began exploring the map of North America. Pyari returned after turning off the gas stove. Nath Ji hid the atlas under a file on the shelf next to the divan.

"When will you have dinner?" asked Pyari.

Nath Ji looked at the TV. An expert was talking about the varieties of manure. "Isn't it too early? It isn't even seven yet."

"Okay. Then I'll warm the meal later."

"What's there for dinner?"

"What we had for lunch. I told you earlier to go and buy some mutton. But you didn't!" Nath Ji gave her a look. She said hesitantly, "You could have had some. I don't enjoy it even though nobody has forbidden me from eating it."

"You used to like it. But of course, this too is my fault. Had I not let it slip that in Paeirgaam, Kaakpoor, and other places . . . in plain sight . . ."

"Please don't remind me of that again. It turns my stomach." Nath Ji noticed Pyari shudder.

Once again, there was a noise at the door. Nath Ji rose abruptly.

Pyari made him sit down. "That's not our door. It's Mir Sahib's."

"How do you know?"

"My eyesight may have weakened, but my hearing is still sharp. I hear doors banging all day long. I should be able to distinguish the sounds they make. I don't sit around at school all day like you."

"I don't give a damn about the school! Being a headmaster is hard work. But I still come back home by two-thirty or three. A minister or an officer might turn up for inspection any day at two-thirty and I would certainly lose my job. It's Kartik Purnima next week. The teachers want to spend the night at Pampore and enjoy the saffron blossoms in the moonlight. But I keep avoiding them."

"Why?"

"What will you do all alone at home?"

Pyari changed the topic, "Get up and latch both the doors. No one will come this late."

Nath Ji had hoped that someone would come to see him that day, some relative or friend or neighbor from the old locality . . . "Today is Saturday, a holiday. Tomorrow is Sunday. Those who want to come will come today. There's no chance tomorrow . . . Who would want to miss *Mahabharat* on TV in the morning or the movie in the afternoon and come to this desolate place? But it looks like no one is going to show up even today . . . I wonder why . . ."

"I say, get up and bolt the doors."

Pyari's voice brought Nath Ji out of his reverie.

"No. Let's wait. Perhaps Gupta Ji from downstairs will come. He had said he might return within a week, and it won't be possible for him to get here from Jammu before eight or nine in the evening."

Pyari accepted this explanation even though she knew it was not true. Before leaving for Amritsar, Gupta Ji had clearly told Nath Ji that he would now return to Kashmir only in March to settle his bills.

"A strange tenant indeed. He has paid for the whole year, but he stays only for fifty or sixty days at the most."

"That's precisely the problem." Nath Ji grabbed the newspaper and spread it out to read.

Pyari continued, "We took a tenant so that he would look after the house, but now apart from taking care of our own house, we also have to guard his belongings. We have become caretakers!"

"Become caretakers?" Nath Ji asked, surprised. When he understood that Pyari was alluding to their absent son, he was outraged. "Don't be stupid. Use your brains!"

Nath Ji advised Pyari to be sensible. But his eyes welled up with tears. He took off his glasses and wiped his eyes. He put the glasses back on and resumed reading. Pyari got up and fetched a big platter of rice from the kitchen. She struggled to clean the rice. It was not bright enough even though the tube light was on. Nath Ji pulled off his glasses again and handed them to his wife who put them on and went back to cleaning the rice. Nath Ji put the newspapers aside and started watching TV. A doctor was talking about diseases that usually affect the elderly. Nath Ji identified with each symptom that the doctor mentioned. He got up and switched off the TV.

Without his newspaper and the TV, Nath Ji became restless and did not know what to do with himself. He wanted to speak to Pyari but she was busy sifting the rice. He started wondering if it had been a good idea to build a house so far away from the city. It was true that the walls of their old house were already crumbling. It wasn't really a house. It was little more than a wattle hut held together only by the grace of God. If a person rolled over at night, the whole house shook. That was why he had not slept with his wife for a long time after they got married. And yet the couple had managed to spend more than fifty years in that rickety wicker bed. What was more, their son Bittĕ was born and brought up in the same house. But when he got a job outside Kashmir after he completed his training, he made it clear that he would not return unless they moved out of that house. Nath Ji had also thought to himself that when Bittĕ got married, it would be embarrassing to bring someone's daughter to live with them in such a wretched place. He had built a two-story house with all his savings and a loan of 75,000 rupees in a place that used to be outside but was now within the city. But Bittĕ did not get married, nor did he come back to live in Kashmir. A few years earlier, he had come back for a month. Last year, he came for only seventeen days . . . And this year? It was two months since Bittĕ had left for Canada. Only God knew when he would return, if at all.

"Should I heat up the food?" Pyari was done sifting the rice. She removed the glasses and returned them to Nath Ji.

"Let's listen to the news first." Nath Ji put on the glasses and opened the newspaper. He started to listen to the news on TV and read the headlines in the newspaper at the same time. By the time he was done with the news in Kashmiri and Urdu and with browsing through pages one, three, five, nine and ten, Pyari had made his bed on the divan and her own on the floor.

"There's no reason for you to make that second bed," Nath Ji spoke hesitantly. "You could sleep in the same bed as me."

"Have you gone mad?" Pyari lost her temper. Nath Ji slapped his forehead. "You never understand what I'm saying. What I meant was making two beds every day involves washing two quilt covers, two pillow cases, two sets of bed sheets every few days. Do you have the strength for all that? If you slept in my bed, your work would be halved."

"Enough! I've heard you!" Her reply reminded Nath Ji of the

Pyari from more than twenty years ago and took him back to a different time altogether. "I said I'm going to heat up the food. How late can we eat?"

"Heat it up then . . . Let's get it done with," said Nath Ji. He muttered to himself, "Let us stay up all night . . . Who cares?"

After dinner, Pyari washed the dishes. Nath Ji was still listening to the news from Delhi when she came out of the kitchen.

"Still up?"

"Why would I sleep so early?"

"At least get into bed. You will feel warmer."

Nath Ji got up, turned off the TV and got into bed with a file in his hand.

"Should I switch off the lights?" Pyari asked.

"Yes. I'll turn on the table lamp. I have to go through some school papers."

Pyari turned off the tube light. Nath Ji switched on the lamp and started going through the pages in the file.

"You stay up! I'm dead tired," Pyari said and went to bed.

"Of course, you're tired. Washing two quilts, covers, and heaps of clothes is no joke."

Pyari turned her back on Nath Ji. Nath Ji did not understand whether she was sleepy or whether she was ignoring him. He closed the file gently and pulled out the atlas he had hidden earlier. Once again, he began to study the map of North America. This is Canada and this is its capital Ottawa . . . And that is Halifax, where Bittĕ must be at the moment. It's not far from Ottawa and is right on the coast

. . . Although it's far north, the weather must be pleasant, just like in Bombay. That's good. Bittĕ is sensitive to cold. And like Bombay, the lights must always be shining across the bay!

It struck Nath Ji that something was wrong with him . . . Why did he think of lights glimmering across a dark sea all the time? Was it because he liked lights, electric bulbs, the first rays of the rising sun shining in a wide-open sky, the warm sunshine spreading across the landscape? Maybe he wanted to experience all of this but couldn't because all of it was on the other side and he was on this side. In between lay this endless sea of darkness.

"Asleep already? And you were wondering what you would do so early in bed," Pyari's voice jolted him out of his reverie. He had actually dozed off.

"Get up, someone just opened the door! You leave the doors unbolted day and night. I wonder which one of your well-wishers you're expecting. As if people have nothing to do but to chat with you. Get up! Why aren't you getting up? You want robbers to loot us?"

Pyari had got out of her bed and was moving about the room restlessly.

"Maybe Guptaji has actually turned up." Nath Ji picked up his torch and went down the stairs. Pyari mustered up some courage, opened the window a little and peered out through the crack. She could make out a couple of shadows in the dark. One was short but wide and the other was tall and slim. When she heard her husband say, "Shoo! Shoo! May the plague strike you!" she relaxed, closed the window, and went back to bed.

Nath Ji chased the cows away, latched the outer gate and the main door and came back to the room. "Doesn't anybody watch over these cows?" said Pyari "They roam about all night! The man who milks them in the morning – why doesn't he bother to see where they go in the evening?"

"If these cows gave milk, they wouldn't be let loose," Nath Ji sighed. "They're starving and that's made them dry and unproductive. That's why they have been abandoned."

Pyari sighed.

"Fortunately, this year it's rained enough," Nath Ji continued. "Last year's drought sent the costs of hay skyrocketing, and that forced milkmen and farmers to let their unproductive cattle loose and sell their old bullocks to butchers. That's why in Paeirgaam, Kaakpoor, and Kelar, this abomination is openly displayed in the shops and sold . . ."

Nath Ji bit his tongue but the words had slipped out of his mouth already. He turned towards Pyari apprehensively, but this time too she was shaken and turned pale.

She responded calmly, "Getting them slaughtered by butchers would be doing them a favor. A big favor. Having one's throat slit is better than being abandoned."

Nath Ji sensed Pyari crying underneath her quilt. Quietly, he slid into his bed, switched off the table lamp and pulled the covers over his head.

A Moment of Madness

Does the river Jhelum still roar, or is it now subdued? The Jamuna appears withered all year round, except during the monsoon. Sitting in a bus on the bridge that spanned the river, Jawe Lal recollected an incident from sixty years ago, when he was a child and had probably not even started school. Japanese goods like pencils, electric lamps, and similar items were easily available in the market then. His uncle, Nath, who was older and ahead of him in school, wouldn't buy Japanese pencils that cost only one or two paisa. He would buy Made in England or Made in Germany pencils that cost one or two annas. They were expensive, but more durable. In comparison, Japanese pencils would snap, Japanese lamps would burn out overnight, and so, all Japanese goods had a bad reputation. Jawe Lal remembered how, when this uncle's new bride had sprained her back while fetching a bucket of water from the riverbank, his older sister had said loudly for all to hear, "How disappointing! Despite being so fastidious, Nath has ended up with a bride just like the Japanese goods in the market."

But things were different today. The bridge on the Jamuna was named the Indo-Japanese Friendship Bridge. The costs for the bridge had been borne entirely by Japan and the construction company had also been Japanese. That was why it was strong and beautiful and had been completed in less than the usual time. It took no more than five minutes to cross the Jamuna since the bridge had opened. Earlier, traffic jams would start as soon as one reached the head of the old bridge, making the ordeal of crossing the Jamuna worse than being ferried across the Vaitarna.

He looked at his watch. Only three minutes had passed, and he was almost on the other side. He was in no particular hurry today, but on previous occasions, when the bus would stop in the middle of the road, he would grow restless. Perhaps God was being kind to him today. Despite the usual rush of buses, cars and scooters on the road, there was no traffic jam and he did not feel the need to tear out his hair in frustration.

Jawe Lal had begun to notice God's favors since the day before, when his son Billa had finally telephoned him after seven days. Billa had left for Frankfurt the previous Wednesday at two in the morning. From there, he had to take a connecting flight to his destination. But there had been no news from him until yesterday. For four days, Jawe Lal had waited patiently, thinking that Billa might not have been able to call since it was a new place, and a new company with new rules and regulations. But when there was still no news on the fifth day, he had grown worried. He had convinced his wife not to fret. But that Billa would take a week to adjust to the new place and would only then be able to call to give them his address, phone and fax numbers – Jawe Lal was anxious. He would have called Billa, but there was no number to call. He would have asked for news, but from whom? Finally, he had done what every hopeless person does. He had taken refuge in God and pleaded – if Billa called or if he heard any good news about him, he would give five rupees to charity. When there was still no news from Billa, Jawe Lal thought perhaps the amount was too small. Embarrassed, he acknowledged his stinginess and committed to giving ten rupees. But even with that, there was no phone call on the sixth day. Maybe God was still not happy. Jawe Lal squirmed like a small fish in a frying pan and increased his donation to twenty rupees. God answered his prayers that very day – Billa called in the evening. Jawe Lal was overjoyed when he heard his son's voice, although Billa scolded him and said that he shouldn't have become so anxious – if there had been an accident or some mishap, the TV or the newspapers would have reported it.

The bus stopped. Jawe Lal was startled. But he sighed with relief when he saw that the traffic light was red. It turned green quickly. The bus was now on the Ring Road, which was quite broad and unlikely to experience traffic jams.

Jawe Lal had left home to visit the Hanuman temple in Connaught Place, but he was not going there to offer sweets or prayers to the deity. He had seen dozens of lame, blind, and pockmarked beggars outside the temple on several occasions. He needed to get small change from the priests or from the sweetshop for the two ten-rupee notes he had in his pocket, distribute the change among those poor, unfortunate beggars, and thus, fulfill the promise he had made to God.

Suddenly, he fell forward in his seat. The bus had stopped again. He peered out of the window, and as far as he could see, all the buses, cars, and scooters in front of his bus had also stopped. He looked around at the people sitting near him in the bus, but they were all calm and quiet, as if nothing had happened. Perhaps nothing had happened. He had read in his childhood: 'In Rome, do as the Romans do.' Now, in his old age, he had learned that in Delhi, do as people in Delhi do – ignore whatever is happening around you, stay quiet and mind your own business. He sat silently now and turned his thoughts to what kept him preoccupied night and day ever since he had left Kashmir. He replayed past events in his mind and ruminated on new problems.

Without warning, a young woman got up from her seat and took a good look at the congested traffic on the road. She seemed to make up her mind, and she moved towards the door of the bus. The conductor understood: he opened the door for her, and she stepped out. Jawe Lal noticed her tight jeans, the flimsy short blouse, her broad hips and full bosom, and between the two, her slender waist, as narrow as the Indo-Japanese Friendship Bridge. Watching her get up from her seat and alight quickly from the bus reminded him, most of all, of the young girls who had studied with him in college. Despite their high-heeled sandals and the jaunty scarves swinging from their shoulders, they had not overcome the fear of social censure. The young people these days, on the other hand, had no inhibitions. They made their own decisions. They believed that whatever path they chose would lead them to their goal. He started thinking – Billa had had a good job here, the salary had been decent and there had been the possibility of a promotion as well. But he had quit that job and contracted himself to an American company for three years to work in some unfamiliar country. He remembered when he had been his son's age – after completing his BA and BEd, he had worked as a teacher in a government middle school. He had been offered a headmaster's job for three times the salary at a school in Delhi. But what would he have done with more money? Would he have left his Kashmir for that? His home? But he did have to leave Kashmir as well as his home. He, who would have sacrificed the world for Kashmir, was exiled from his homeland forever in an instant.

Jawe Lal felt like laughing rather than crying as he thought about his misfortunes. He laughed out loud without realizing it. But this made no impression on the other passengers. They had either dozed off or sat with eyes wide open, as if they were frozen. He thought of the girl in jeans and wondered if she had reached her destination. Had Billa been allotted a separate house by his company or was he sharing a shack on-site with the workers? Again, his thoughts turned to Kashmir. Three years ago, he had sworn that he wouldn't think about Kashmir anymore. Just then, the bus started to move. The sudden movement of the bus frightened Jawe Lal, as though it were reminding him that he was breaking a solemn oath and that thinking of Kashmir would cause him harm. Or maybe it was suggesting that being stubborn and deliberately erasing all memory of Kashmir was wrong. Just like the stalled traffic which had begun to move, his stagnant life would be revitalized if he allowed himself to think about Kashmir again.

His bus and all the other stalled vehicles were now moving. He looked out of the window and caught sight of the young girl in the jeans and blouse walking briskly along the road. He saw her in a quick flash. Then, the bus sped away and left her behind. Jawe Lal was convinced that perseverance pays. He had tried very hard to convince Billa of this, but to no avail. It was humiliating to try and persuade a person who was not willing to listen. An impatient man will settle for anything.

After speeding along for a few minutes, the bus suddenly stopped. Again, the traffic came to a standstill. A few more people got off the bus. Jawe Lal looked out of the window. A number of passengers had disembarked from other buses and were walking slowly along the road. He watched them. He spotted the young woman in the jeans and blouse once more. She walked on and left the bus behind. Jawe Lal reconsidered the matter: was patience truly rewarding or did impatience lead a person to success?

As he got off the bus at Regal and walked towards the Hanuman temple, Jawe Lal wondered if the young woman in the jeans and blouse had reached her destination or whether she was still walking along the road. But this was not the right way to think about the problem. The question was not whether the young woman had arrived at her destination. A person may walk or take a flight, but can a destination ever be reached? This was the real question for Jawe Lal, and he certainly did not have an answer.

When he arrived at the Hanuman temple, he grew anxious again. It was not a Tuesday, and though there was a crowd of worshippers, he could not see any beggars. A bystander who looked rather unhinged understood Jawe Lal's anxiety. Jawe Lal found out from him that the beggars had a leader who instructed them to beg outside the Hanuman temple on Tuesday, the Sai Baba temple on Thursday, the Jama Masjid on Friday, the Bhairav temple on Saturday, and the gurdwara on Sunday. They had the day off on Wednesday and Monday. Today was Wednesday. The headman was generous and kind. Like the government, for years now, he too had been following the five-day workweek.

When he heard this, Jawe Lal was able to make sense of something that had happened twelve years ago. He had traveled to Delhi for a five-day trip with a group of ten boys. When he was showing the boys around Raj Ghat, Shantivan and Shakti Sthal, they had encountered a large procession. A president or a minister from some unknown country in Africa or South America had been ousted. Hundreds of poor people in India, barefoot and dressed in rags, holding enormous posters of this politician, were protesting his expulsion as an attack on democracy. Jawe Lal had been surprised. When the boys had asked him who this leader was, where was he from and why were Indians concerned about him, Jawe Lal had no answer. He felt ashamed of his ignorance. Today, he realized that those impoverished people must have been paid to protest for a man who was unknown to them. They had simply come to make some money on a Wednesday or a Monday, their days off.

Jawe Lal left the temple without making an offering of flowers or anything else to the deity. As he headed home with the two ten-rupee notes still in his pocket, he felt he was leaving without having accomplished anything. He walked to the bus stop with his head down and slipped into the bus. He closed his eyes tightly when the bus started. He knew that one could see with one's eyes wide open, but if that didn't help a person to understand his own situation, it was better to keep them shut. However, he was compelled to open his eyes when he got off the bus and had to hire a rickshaw to get home. The rickshaw puller demanded six rupees as the fare. Jawe Lal grew angry, assuming that rickshaw puller saw him as an outsider and was trying to cheat him. He declared that the fare was five rupees and he was not going to pay a paisa more. Faced with Jawe Lal's dogged insistence, the rickshaw puller backed down and agreed to the five-rupee fare. But he compelled Jawe Lal to listen to the account of his miserable life. The man was from Bihar and had come to Delhi to make a living. Jawe Lal felt that, like himself, the rickshaw puller too was a displaced person. But when the rickshaw puller revealed that he had chosen to leave his village and come to the big city to earn better money, Jawe Lal was reminded more of his son Billa. The rickshaw puller ranted on about unemployment, forced labour and gut-wrenching hunger. Jawe Lal's mind went blank. His heart beat wildly, and he felt as if he were being tossed up one mountain and thrown down another, ferried across the gushing Jhelum and flung into the dried-up Jamuna. Like a drowning man, he raised both his hands and was about to cry out to Billa for help. But Billa was far away, across many oceans.

Jawe Lal stopped the rickshaw when he reached home and gave the man five rupees. The man pleaded for one more rupee. Firmly, Jawe Lal said that he was not going to pay more than what they had agreed upon and stepped out of the rickshaw. The rickshaw driver gave up on this obstinate passenger and was about to leave when Jawe Lal called him back. He stopped. Jawe Lal took the two ten-rupee notes from his pocket, put the money in the rickshaw puller's hand without a word, and walked towards his house.

The rickshaw puller examined the notes carefully. Both were genuine and in good shape, neither torn nor wrinkled. He was taken aback by the inexplicable behavior of the passenger who had seemed so miserly but now had given him two crisp ten-rupee notes.

To Rage or to Endure

I WAS ACCUSTOMED TO SOFT, WHITE, COTTONY SNOW. IN THE LATE autumn months, Dĕd, my grandmother, would start worrying that Shēnĕ-Buddĕ – Old Man Snow – would show up any day. And so, she would dry garlands of sliced gourd and aubergine in the sun in advance of his arrival. I didn't know if she intended to adorn the old man with these garlands, or huddle in a corner and satisfy her own appetite. I could never figure out whether she loved the snow or dreaded it.

Dĕd would complain – and perhaps rightly so – that snow is cold. As for me, the very sight of it gave me the feeling of warmth that comes from quilts filled with freshly carded cotton. My brother moved out of our house soon after he got married. My sister-in-law would not make garlands of gourd and aubergine to welcome

Shēnĕ-Buddĕ or to guard herself against him. She would call the carder at the end of the lane over and get him to tease out cotton from her worn-out quilts before filling them again. Then, she would get the tailor's apprentice from across the road to make snow-white covers for these quilts. My sister-in-law's intelligence and the skills of the carder and the tailor made me think that this is how one should prepare to welcome the snow. Dĕd's lack of preparedness and my own naiveté made me feel sorry for myself. But when the snow fell heavily, I rejoiced at the thought that there was a carder up in the sky far more skilled than the one at the end of the lane, who carded tonnes of cotton for my quilts and mattresses. No human craftsman could match that master craftsman who cut bales of snow-white cloth to make pristine covers for these quilts.

I enjoyed lying in quilts of cotton-soft snow and stepping on mattresses of snow. As soon as my feet touched it, they sank in. I imagined my sister-in-law's plump body and her fair limbs sinking similarly, being caressed by soft quilts and mattresses.

"Quilts and mattresses are soft as well as warm. But snow, though it's soft, freezes quickly and feels colder," said Dĕd, flaunting her wisdom. I did not take her seriously, for I believed that there could be nothing in the universe as cold and frozen as old, worn-out quilts and mattresses.

Days, months, and years kept passing and it kept snowing. What is colder, snow or old worn-out rags? Though we disagreed about this intensely, Dĕd and I continued to support each other. I grew up, even as Dĕd grew old.

That year, too, Děd made garlands of dried gourd and aubergine to welcome Shēnĕ-Buddĕ, or to guard herself against him. That year, too, it snowed heavily. The snow danced as it fell from the sky, but as soon as it touched the ground it went into a frenzy. Or perhaps a gust of wind came in from somewhere and struck the soft flakes descending from the sky, turning them into ice, freezing them just as they hit the ground. The soft heaps of cotton turned to frost, and the bales of white cloth turned into crystals. Neither Děd nor I was accustomed to this. An icy wind blew that pierced the flesh and bones, and froze the warm blood that ran through people's veins before they even realized what had hit them. They could have grasped it only if they had been used to it. When I saw this cruel face of Shēnĕ-Buddĕ and was confronted by the icy winds, I let out a scream and Děd screamed even louder. But none of our neighbors heard us. Perhaps even our screams froze before they could reach their ears.

Děd held me tight and started howling. I lifted her on my back and turned towards the door. Děd glanced around the house, gathering the images of the garlands of gourd and aubergine hanging in the attic, the pots and pans lying about in the rooms and corridors, and bundled them away in her heart. Perhaps my heart was already frozen. The plates covered in mold, the earthenware with iced-on collard greens, the frozen pitcher, the horoscope trapped in unfavorable planetary combinations, the almanac stamped with ominous dates – I kicked it all away to clear a path in front of us.

As soon as I stepped out of the door with Děd, I slipped. We kept rolling down the icy slopes until we reached a place we did not recognize. The cotton-soft snow had held my feet to its chest and caressed them gently, but this frozen snow could not bear our weight even for a second. It hurled us to the ground and we skidded on its slippery surface, tumbling down countless slopes, through gorges and crevasses, until we reached a place where the sky above was on fire and the sand below blazed like an oven.

"Is there any one around?" Děd yelled again. But just like before, no one came to help us.

She sighed.

I tried to tell her, "Who will come to help us here? In this endless desert, we are like two grains of sand, almost non-existent. In the scope of this universe, you and I are just two dots . . . two points . . ."

"What is a point?" she asked.

"A point is a sign that does not have length, breadth or height, but to identify it we call it *alif bey* or *a b* or *ka kha*. These names only have meaning when they are placed in a matrix defined by three lines. We are adrift because we have lost our grip on this matrix. Though our ribs didn't break when we tumbled down the slopes, we lost track of the coordinates that gave meaning to our existence."

"So, even here, there is no one we can call our own?" That is what Děd gleaned from my ramblings.

"No one, except this Sun, who himself is on fire up in the sky," I responded.

"What good will he do me? I would be grateful if he would just set."

The Sun heard Děd's words. Perhaps it is only someone who is burning who can understand the pain of others. He began to share his own helplessness. "Am I free to rise and light the skies on fire? If I were, I would also have the freedom to set and vanish when it pleased me! If it were up to me, do you think I would be hanging in the middle of the sky, scorching others as well as myself?"

I couldn't accept this. So I said to the Sun: "What are you saying? You can't decide when to set?"

"What makes you think that I am the same sun you were accustomed to?"

"What else are you?"

"I travel through the skies, but I am not Tulsidas's rising sun, the one who destroyed the rakshasas and created the ideal world. I am a kite borne on a fragile thread and handed over to the winds of time, so that they can do with me as they please. But suddenly, the wind itself died down and left me stranded in the middle of the sky."

"Why doesn't the one who sent you up there like a kite reel you back in and put you out of your misery?"

"Who knows what happened to the old man who dreamt of the ideal world? He persuaded so many people to spin thread. He had great faith in the hand-spun thread which turned out to be actually quite fragile . . . This thread snapped and now I am stranded . . ."

"Was that old man Shēnĕ-Buddĕ?" Dĕd asked.

"No, Shēnĕ-Buddĕ's hair and beard are white as snow. But the old man who left me stranded was bald and clean shaven."

"God knows who that old man was . . . But what kind of a person relies on fragile threads?"

The Sun turned to Děd and retorted, "Dědi, they say that in olden times there once was a Děd like you, in your homeland, who spun a thread finer than anyone else. She had such faith in this fragile thread that she used it to ferry her boat across the sea. Like Děd, my old man must have believed that his fragile thread was stronger than iron chains. He told people, 'Hold on fast to this thread. If God hears your plea, he will take you across.' But people thought the old man was talking rubbish. They laughed so loudly, my thread broke into bits and I was left stranded in the middle of nowhere . . . I smoulder, but I don't turn to ash. People burn, yet they rage. They endure. They become used to fire and the blazing sun. You rage because you were used to snow and shade."

Who knows if Děd understood all this. But I realized that there are only two paths in front of us: to endure or to rage . . . Děd will last only a few more moments. But I have to live a long life. I have nothing to gain from rage. I must endure and adapt. Perhaps I have already begun to do so.

Glossary

Ab ke savan ghar aa A lyrical song in Hindi.

Achkan The name of a traditional knee-length coat worn by men in South Asia.

Anna A unit of money not currently used. There are sixteen annas in a rupee.

Batta A colloquial name for Kashmiri Pandits. Depending on the context, it can also be invoked as a derogatory term.

Congress and Janata Two main political parties.

Jal Tarang A percussion instrument.

Jināb A polite form of address.

Kakin A name used for elderly women or mothers in Pandit households in Kashmir. Mataji would be more recognizable across India, therefore more cosmopolitan.

Kāngĕr A wicker basket with a clay pot filled with hot embers. A Kashmiri heater.

Keema Any form of ground meat.

Khan Sahib hamare saath piyo. Khan Sahib, please drink with us. (Original is in Urdu.)

Lal Děd (1320-1392) was a mystic and poet whose verses are among the earliest compositions in the Kashmiri language.

Mleccha A derogatory term used for outsiders. Can denote people from different religions or castes.

Paan The Betel leaf native to South Asia often used as a breath freshener.

Phěrăn A traditional Kashmiri gown worn by men and women.

Shalwar-kameez A knee length tunic with pleated trousers worn by both men and women in South Asia.

Sheikh Abdullah (1905-1982) was a political leader from the Kashmir valley who founded All Jammu and Kashmir National Conference in the 1930s. He was the first prime minister of the state after accession of Kashmir to India.

Sherwani The name of a traditional knee-length coat worn by men in South Asia.

Shiva Mahimna Stotra An important hymn to Lord Shiva.

Thumri A light form of Hindustani classical music.

Yakhni A traditional Kashmiri meat dish cooked with yogurt.

Translator's Note

KAUL'S SHORT STORIES ARE IN AND OF THEMSELVES A PLEASURE to read. However, like much great literature, they also make us uncomfortable. Kaul forces us to think about difficult social questions – particularly the troubled political relationship between individuals, communities, and nations that collide in Kashmir. He addresses their anxieties and perceptions, the values they share and those that divide them; he delineates the ethical conundrums of individuals wedged in power relations. Kaul's depiction of people is not static. He deftly traces movement and transformation – traces the subtle changes in the emotional and political consciousness of his subjects and the tragic unraveling of a place he calls home: Kashmir.

While at times he makes use of phantasmagoric devices, his primary concerns are earthbound, everyday and human. The persuasive power of his writing can largely be attributed to the situations and personalities through which he articulates his moral vision. These are immediately recognizable and intimately accessible to his Kashmiri readers. While he brings us face to face with our own myopia, his incisive wit and humor ensure that we do not escape his scrutiny – even as he systematically disembowels what we tend to downplay out of propriety or expediency, those secret desires we rarely dare to acknowledge even to ourselves.

Unlike a partisan trend in contemporary Kashmiri writing – particularly in English – that victimizes a community, demonizing the other while valorizing the self, Kaul subverts the binaries of good and evil, friend and enemy, self and other. Delving into the messiness of our private and public selves with disarming honesty, he sheds light on social and psychic pathos with meticulous detail often missing from political commentary and other kinds of writing on Kashmir.

Just as there is a difficulty in finding words following a traumatic experience, writing after experiencing political uncertainty and social disorder does not come easily. It involves a slow processing and reworking of trauma. It is as though, in an attempt to articulate the unspeakable and make it accessible to the mind, words seek to suture the damage to the social and psychic fabric. Without belittling the immensity of the task by rushing through the process – or the opposite, accentuating or perpetuating pain as a pathology or toward some political end – Kaul makes multiple attempts at social recovery and healing. He avoids direct references to violence and death in his accounts of trauma. The harsher the reality becomes, the more he resorts to symbolic language. The bitterness of harsh moments is tempered with a deft use of irony and humor, myth and metaphor. Kaul harnesses cultural tropes: legends and myths, figures and places that have acquired a timeless quality in an attempt to recreate a meaningful present out of the ashes of the recent past.

The orality that pervades much of Kaul's work provides direct access to social situations. His stories lend themselves to an array of interpretations. This dynamic, open-ended quality of Kaul's writing is difficult to retain in translation. The translator must pay attention to the cultural and political nuances of the language. A close reading of the text can potentially unsettle emotional, historical, and political realities – in other words, the officially held order of things in Kashmir. Therein lies the true creative genius and subversive potential of Kaul's oeuvre. His stories recover a nuanced multifaceted history of a crucial period of political transition and rupture in Kashmir (1970–2000) that lacks a social history.

Gowhar Fazili

Translator's Note

AT THE END OF THE TUMULTUOUS 1940S, KASHMIRIS FREED themselves from a century-long feudal rule. The Progressive Writers Movement* had already made inroads into the cultural sphere of Kashmir early in the decade. It further aided the fight against the Dogra rule by providing it with a creative stimulus.

---

* The Progressive Writers' Association was formed in Kashmir in 1947 with Ghulam Muhammad Sadiq, the influential political leader of the time, as its first patron. Its founding members were inspired by the Progressive Writers' Movement of the undivided India, whose members had contacted and met poets and writers in Srinagar. Like their Indian counterparts, the members of the Progressive Writers' Association of Kashmir had their ideological roots anchored in Communism.

Kashmiris looked forward to an equitable society with a vision of liberty and prosperity. The new political dispensation recruited from the ranks of the Progressives, who were at the forefront of the fight for liberation. But when the promised reforms were implemented in the early 1950s, the socioeconomic inequities of the past continued as the ruling elites of society remained firmly in place. The vision of liberty and happiness turned into a scenario of anger, terror and distrust. As the situation grew darker, disillusionment grew widespread. People watched professed proponents of Progressive thought switch sides and topple a popular government lead by Sheikh Abdullah in 1953. This monumental betrayal would have far-reaching and devastating consequences.

The Progressive ideology that held sway over Kashmir began to lose its grip. Literature and literary criticism that had been couched in ideological rhetoric to create a political consciousness among the people started to lose its potency. In the 1960s, the Kashmiri literary fraternity split into two antagonistic factions. One group turned its attention to the complexities of everyday life. This generation of writers advanced a range of radical new ideas. Their familiarity with the writings of Balzac, Chekhov, Maupassant, and Tolstoy, among others, inspired them to move beyond idealistic limitations. This allowed them to rediscover what they already had but which had escaped recognition and appreciation in literature. But it wasn't easy to represent everyday realities in literature. It was akin to Impressionist painters dispensing with studio practices and depicting in their work the transient effects of what they saw, felt and thought.

The desire to represent life in its raw forms gradually heralded a subversion in language. Poets and writers blended spoken language with the written word to capture life and its realities in Kashmir. The first writer of this new sensibility with a distinct flair for the short story was Akhter Mohiuddin (1928–2001), who wrote with quite conscious aplomb. Hari Krishna Kaul was among the group of writers who followed in Mohiuddin's footsteps. Kaul's notable contemporaries included Amin Kamil, Bansi Nirdosh, Deepak Kaul, Ali Mohammad Lone, Taj Begum, Ghulam Nabi Shakir, and Ghulam Nabi Baba, among others.

In a career spanning over three decades, Kaul transformed the quotidian into fiction and excelled in portraying the vicissitudes of the world with matchless understanding, insight, wit, compassion and veracity. Kaul unequivocally shared the dismay at the political uncertainties and large-scale social devastations of his time. The point of his writing, however, was not to contest this reality. It was to reveal various situations in their complexity and richness to show how much more there was to lose. Not assuming the inclusive character of Kashmiri society, Kaul in his stories excavated the strengths that bound it together, while also exposing the fault lines that lurked behind its cultural veneer. Both these aspects lay hidden beneath layers of the commonplace. Therefore, Kaul structured his narratives as excavations that reveal the web of reality beneath the surface. His frameless representations of Kashmiri society are sometimes so real that one can touch them. Kaul exposes the contentious issues deeply ingrained in the Kashmiri psyche. Communal slurs are yet another example of this divide where speech can become another form of violence. Kaul is not shy when using the many Kashmiri slurs in his stories that Muslims and Pandits reserve for one another. He uses humor and slang in a Freudian sense to reveal what is suppressed or forbidden by society. Surprisingly, his earlier translators and Kaul himself eschewed both when translating the stories into English and Hindi.

In his position as the dispassionate narrator of many of his stories, it is difficult to tell where Kaul stood vis-à-vis the Kashmiri society of his time. He mainly positions himself as a raconteur at a distance. For instance, in *A Song of Despair*, he is the sleepless narrator sitting on a window ledge to escape the humidity of the night. While doing so, he witnesses a story that takes place inside a house across the lane. In stories written in the first person, such as "That Which We Cannot Speak Of" and "For Now, It Is Night," Kaul depicts himself as a chronicler of events without taking a clear position, ending with conjectures. Weaving multiple strands of thought together in "That Which We Cannot Speak Of," Kaul seems about to assume a position but instead ends the story abruptly, though not without acknowledging the repercussions of speaking about matters for which silence was an unwritten dictum. Intriguingly, "That Which We Cannot Speak Of" begins with a legend and ends with a direct reference to a watershed moment in Kashmir's modern political history. The year was 1931. In the collective memory of Kashmiris, this year exists as the beginning of a concerted resistance movement against Dogra rule that ended in 1947. Kaul, however, traces the roots of fear, insecurity and apprehension of the Kashmiri Pandit community to the arson and looting that took place in a part of the old city in Srinagar during the 1931 uprising. The community was targeted for being in cahoots with the feudal system. In "That Which We Cannot Speak Of," Kaul provides an unrivaled impression of the currents and contradictions of the Pandit community in the events that followed this lesser-known episode of history.

In the same story, Kaul explores the multiple sociopolitical and communal conflicts that both communities had to navigate in order to negotiate a shared social space. He has captured the overt resentment of the majority against the minority for their allegiance to the powers at the helm. He also sees the bitterness and dislike the minority community harbored against the majority, albeit uttered only *sotto voce* in private. These examples suggest that Kaul did not keep himself from acknowledging that evil exists and often triumphs. He, however, had little interest in confronting it. He preferred through his stories to create a space for escape. But escape is not a means for redemption. Instead, it is a specific way of being. It possesses depth and contains layers of meaning not immediately visible to an unaccustomed eye.

In the stories written after the migration of Pandits in 1989, Kaul maps the territories of his memory. Now that the distant narrator is physically estranged from his native place, he is left to oscillate between the self and its true home. Writing becomes a way to escape from the present and to seek refuge in the imaginations of what has been left behind forever. It becomes a way to overcome the crippling sorrow of loss and to reconcile with a life outside the habitual order. The more he tries to get used to it, the more unsettling the experience becomes. Kaul attempts to articulate the insurmountable sadness of exile in "To Rage Or To Endure," which he wrote in the aftermath of displacement. In a significant departure from his writing style, Kaul resorts to metaphor to make sense of the forced rift between himself and his native place. Back home, his contemporaries were dumbstruck by the political events that ruptured Kashmir in 1989. An invisible war had pushed them into a sullen silence. The directness of expression that was the hallmark of writers of Kaul's generation was replaced with esoteric language and themes that shared no affinity with the nightmarish situation. For both Kaul and his compatriots in Kashmir, language had yet again failed to express the horrors of reality.

Like any good writer, Kaul is many things – often a contradictory and complex mixture of things. But he is almost never boring – and certainly not in the stories offered here. The splendid blend of spoken and written language provides a translator with an exceptionally rich source of images and registers. All four of us have attempted to capture the richness and depth of Kaul's stories to render them comprehensible within the framework of the English language. Yet, despite our best efforts to remain faithful to the source text – and equally just to the target language – there is much to lament about what has fallen through the cracks.

Tanveer Ajsi

YALI

The translations in this volume have been mentored and financially supported by the Yali Project at Sangam House.

The Yali Project at Sangam House nurtures and mentors translators and translations in and out of Indian languages. Through its network of editors and publishers, Yali strives to ensure that these translations are published and are widely disseminated.

Yali seeks to build a community of translators, foreground translations lists at publishing houses, and increase the awareness and appreciation of works from Indian languages both at home and abroad.